MY SCOTLAND

The following titles are all in the *Fonthill Complete A. G. Macdonell* Series.
The year indicates when the first edition was published.
See **www.fonthillmedia.com** for details.

Fiction

England, their England (1933)
How Like an Angel   (1934)
Lords and Masters   (1936)
The Autobiography of a Cad   (1939)
Flight From a Lady   (1939)
Crew of the Anaconda   (1940)

Short Stories

The Spanish Pistol   (1939)

Non-Fiction

Napoleon and his Marshals   (1934)
A Visit to America   (1935)
My Scotland   (1937)

Crime and Thrillers written under the pseudonym of John Cameron

The Seven Stabs   (1929)
Body Found Stabbed   (1932)

Crime and Thrillers written under the pseudonym of Neil Gordon

The New Gun Runners (1928)
The Factory on the Cliff   (1928)
The Professor's Poison (1928)
The Silent Murders   (1929)
The Big Ben Alibi   (1930)
Murder in Earl's Court (1931)
The Shakespeare Murders   (1933)

MY SCOTLAND

A. G. MACDONELL

FONTHILL

The original 1937 edition was dedicated by Macdonell

TO MY MOTHER

Fonthill Media Limited
Fonthill Media LLC
www.fonthillmedia.com
office@fonthillmedia.com

First published 1937
This edition published in the United Kingdom 2012

British Library Cataloguing in Publication Data:
A catalogue record for this book is available from the British Library

Copyright © in Introduction, Fonthill Media 2012

ISBN 978-1-78155-031-1 (print)
ISBN 978-1-78155-064-9 (e-book)

Typeset in 10pt on 13pt Sabon
Printed and bound in England

Contents

List of Illustrations

This eclectic selection of illustrations is as chosen by Macdonell for the 1937 edition.

Introduction to the 2012 Edition

Alan Sutton

What a strange county we live in — if, that is, the United Kingdom can be called a country. Are we a nation, or are we several nations? Ten years ago, if one asked an Englishmen of his nationality, the answer would usually come, 'British'. To ask a Scotsman the same question has, since the first act of union in 1707, nearly always derived the answer, 'Scottish', but perhaps nowadays with growing emphasis. The ancient national spirit is rising and now Englishmen too will mostly answer, 'English'. Undoubtedly, the invention of the United Kingdom of Great Britain and Northern Ireland is a mess, an historic fudge that few can define correctly in any detail. Few writers, however, have attacked the union with quite such vitriol as A. G. Macdonell, calling it in his Foreword of *My Scotland*, a 'rather stale music-hall joke'. And few, least of all the original publishers Jarrold & Co., would have expected such invective against the 'incalculable' English to spring from the pen of the author of *England, Their England*, a charming, gentle satire and Macdonell's masterpiece.

Archibald Gordon Macdonell — Archie — was born on 3 November 1895 in Poona, India, the younger son of William Robert Macdonell of Mortlach, a prominent merchant in Bombay, and Alice Elizabeth, daughter of John Forbes White, classical scholar and patron of the arts. It seems likely that Archie was named after Brevet-Colonel A. G. Macdonell, CB, presumably an uncle, who commanded a force that defeated Sultan Muhammed Khan at the fort of Shabkader in the Afghan campaign of 1897.

The family left India in 1896 and Archie was brought up at 'Colcot' in Enfield, Middlesex, and the Macdonell family home of 'Bridgefield', Bridge of Don, Aberdeen. He was educated at Horris Hill preparatory school near Newbury, and Winchester College, where he won a scholarship. Archie left school in 1914, and two years later, he joined the Royal Field Artillery of the 51st Highland Division as a second lieutenant. His experiences fighting on the Western Front were to have a great influence on the rest of his life.

The 51st, known by the Germans as the 'Ladies from Hell' on account of their kilts, were a renowned force, boasting engagements at Beaumont-Hamel, Arras, and Cambrai. But by the time of the 1918 Spring Offensives, the division was war-worn and under strength; it suffered heavily and Archie Macdonell was invalided back to England, diagnosed with shell shock.

After the war, Macdonell worked with the Friends' Emergency and War Victims Relief Committee, a Quaker mission, on reconstruction in eastern Poland and famine in Russia. Between 1922 and 1927 he was on the headquarters staff of the League of Nations Union, which has prominent mention in *Flight from a Lady* (1939) and *Lords and Masters* (1936). In the meantime he stood unsuccessfully as Liberal candidate for Lincoln in the general elections of 1923 and '24. On 31 August 1926, Macdonell married Mona Sabine Mann, daughter of the artist Harrington Mann and his wife, Florence Sabine Pasley. They had one daughter, Jennifer. It wasn't a happy marriage and they divorced in 1937, Mona citing her husband's adultery.

A. G. Macdonell began his career as an author in 1927 writing detective stories, sometimes under the pseudonyms Neil Gordon or John Cameron. He was also highly regarded at this time as a pugnacious and perceptive drama critic; he frequently contributed to the *London Mercury*, a literary journal founded in 1919 by John Collings Squire, the poet, writer, and journalist, and Archie's close friend.

By 1933 Macdonell had produced nine books, but it was only with the publication in that year of *England, Their England* that he truly established his reputation as an author. A gentle, affectionate satire of eccentric English customs and society, *England, Their England* was highly praised and won the prestigious James Tait Black Award in 1933. Macdonell capitalized on this success with another satire, *How Like an Angel* (1934), which parodied the 'bright young things' and the British legal system. The military history *Napoleon and his Marshals* (1934) signalled a new direction; although Macdonell thought it poorly rewarded financially, the book was admired by military experts and it illustrated the range of his abilities. Between 1933 and 1941, A. G. Macdonell produced eleven more books, including the superlative *Lords and Masters* (1936), which tore into 1930s upper-class hypocrisy in a gripping and prescient thriller, and *The Autobiography of a Cad* (1939), an hilarious mock-memoir of one Edward Fox-Ingleby, ruthless landowner, unscrupulous politician, and consummate scoundrel.

My Scotland was first published in 1937, having been commissioned by Jarrold & Co. to sit alongside the cosy titles of *My Wales* by Rhys Davies and *My Ireland* by Edward Dunsany. The Jarrold commissioning editor must have rubbed his hands with glee when Archie Macdonell accepted the commission, reflecting on the success of *England Their England*. Upon receipt of the manuscript, however, it's likely that his feelings changed dramatically. At the very start, Macdonell outlines his assessment of Scotland, linked intractably, in his opinion, to England:

> Briefly, what I think is that it [Scotland] has suffered in the past, and is suffering now, from too much England. The choice before Scotland today is whether in the future to suffer from less England, or from still more. Nothing remains static. In this book I am trying to give my reasons for thinking that Scotland would do well to suffer from less.

Macdonell was educated in England, he fought for Great Britain in the First World War, he moved in English literary circles, and spent most of his working life in London. The root of his extraordinary animosity towards the English is hard to trace. Personal stress surrounding his concurrent divorce in 1937 could have contributed to a vindictive mood; teasing suffered at school and among literary contemporaries could have, perhaps, built up resentment, although as a satirist, he was more than capable of understanding the Englishman's fondness for a harmless joke (however, the writer Alec Waugh did describe Macdonell as 'delightful … but quarrelsome and choleric'); or perhaps his ire against the English was born of nothing other than his Scottish blood, burning for some sort of justice for past crimes, or at the very least, a humble acknowledgement of those crimes. He notes early on that the Englishman's brotherly affection towards the Scotsman is a matter of extreme irritation:

> The only flicker of the old spirit of Bruce and Wallace has shone in the annual international golf-match against England. Here a deep and passionate resolve to defeat the enemy of centuries animates the Scots. Here for a moment the superiority complex is forgotten. Here a fiery breath of hostility sweeps over the links, and, as a rule, the English are beaten. It must be admitted, however, that it is not simply a patriotic fervour on the one side that produces this result. There is also a contributory lack of intense seriousness on the other. The Scots are fighting Bannockburn over again; the English are having a pleasant day's golf. The Scots are desperately anxious to win; the English want to play well — who does not? — and do not much care who is the winner. It need hardly be added that this attitude of bland and slightly cynical indifference maddens the Scots almost beyond endurance. There are few things more exasperating than an adversary who treats a contest which involves national honour as if it were a mere game, as, of course, it is.

But there is no hint of reluctant admiration for the infuriating English. Macdonell declares that the steps that led them to achieve any measure of greatness were merely 'flashes of genius', bewildering occurrences that sprung miraculously from an otherwise brutish and primitive society.

> Why should a nation which is and always has been only faintly educated, produce the greatest list of poets since the days of Athens? Why should a nation which is probably in all apparent essentials the stupidest in Western Europe invariably succeed in any undertaking of any magnitude? Why should a nation which prides itself upon its placidity, its good-nature, and its sportsmanship lose its temper so badly when it is frightened, and commit such atrocities when the cause for fright has been removed? Why again should the same nation display an almost poetical insight into the characters of other nations when its bad temper has died down?

In battle, the Scots could not match the wealth and resources of the English; the union was formed and Highland regiments were established in the British Army. In 1937, Macdonell saw the Scottish acceptance of the status quo as shameful and wrong; feelings echoed today by Alex Salmond's Scottish National Party. Macdonell's conclusion is unequivocal and provocative:

> Fundamentally, there is no half-way house between freedom and slavery. In the end there is no such thing as a free and enlightened provincialism. There can never be a partnership on equal terms between a small partner and an overwhelmingly strong one. The former must inevitably be absorbed in the end.
>
> That is what is happening to Scotland today, and the process must either be accelerated or reversed. There is not the slightest use pretending that Scotland can survive in its present position. It is all very well for the ostrich to hide its head in the sand, but we Scots ought to remember what happens to the ostrich. He ends up in a farm where his owner plucks out his feathers and makes money by selling them.

It would be interesting to know where Macdonell would stand in today's political climate. It seems he failed to appreciate that the status of the other partner in the union — England — may change over the years, thus affecting the balance of power. 'Slavery' seems an absurd word to use nowadays, but the sentiment is not far from that being expressed by Alex Salmond and his party. Perhaps one day we shall find *My Scotland* on the Scottish national curriculum.

In 1940, three years after the publication of *My Scotland*, Macdonell married his second wife, Rose Paul-Schiff, a Viennese whose family was connected with the banking firm of Warburg Schiff. His health had been weak since the First World War, and he died suddenly of heart failure in his Oxford home on 16 January 1941, at the age of 45.

J. B. Morton of *Beachcomber* fame remembered his friend Archie Macdonell as a man of conviction, with a 'sense of compassion for every kind of unhappiness'. Out of character *My Scotland* may be, but none other of Macdonell's works come close to illustrating this description so convincingly. Rarely has a book demonstrated such conviction in the unshakable certainty that the English are to blame for all of Scotland's misfortunes and that freedom within Great Britain is but an illusion. *My Scotland* is also a compassionate lament for an intensely proud nation beaten into loathsome submission.

From the first word of the title, *My Scotland* is personal. It is biased, opinionated and, at times, factually questionable, but it is undeniably impassioned. And yet, after the book's publication, Macdonell continued to live in London, among the enemy. Perhaps it was shame that drove him to write so scathingly about the country that nurtured him as a writer — shame for his own personal benefit from the bloody union. Whatever the case, seventy-five years on, *My Scotland* remains an ardent and topical exposition of Scottish nationalism; it is an important part of the Fonthill A. G. Macdonell series.

Foreword

This is not an expert book. It is not an historical, economic, or sociological treatise. Nor is it a description of the scenery of Scotland. Mr H. V. Morton is not a man in whose footsteps anyone can follow. It is simply an attempt to write down what I think about my native country.

Briefly, what I think is that it has suffered in the past, and is suffering now, from too much England. The choice before Scotland today is whether in the future to suffer from less England, or from still more. Nothing remains static. In this book I am trying to give my reasons for thinking that Scotland would do well to suffer from less. That is my own opinion and naturally I want others to share it.

I have been moved to this opinion only gradually. But though the process has been slow it has been complete. I am now convinced that Scotsmen must decide in the near future whether they wish to be citizens of a free country or citizens of a rather stale music-hall joke. And I am quite certain that no middle course is possible. The English are so strong in their powers of assimilation that sooner or later an equal partnership, assuming that such a thing had ever existed, must become impossible. It was against these powers that the Irish fought so long and in the end so successfully.

It was against them that the Lowlands of Scotland fought until 1707. Either we must resume the fight where it was left off or else we must gracefully accept assimilation. To those who agree with my arguments and conclusions I offer my hand, to those who do not, my condolences.

Mr George Blake has written in his book, *The Heart of Scotland*:

> "it is simply necessary for practical purposes to take the conventional view of Scotland as consisting of two regions, differently peopled, the Highlands and the Lowlands. To take Scotland thus in black and white is neither good history nor good geography. There would be reason in regarding the industrial belt as a corridor apart or a melting-pot of all the elements in the country. But as the

Lowland tradition tends to prevail in that thickly populated area (with some queer and charming exceptions that will be duly noted) the rough division is permissible and useful."

Throughout this book I have followed Mr Blake's example (for anyone writing about Scotland what better or wiser example could there be?) and used the words Highlander and Lowlander to mean, broadly, what we all know they mean, broadly, when we use them in everyday speech.

* * *

There is one question which has to be answered at once, before any book about Scotland can be begun. What is Scotland? Is it a land of one race, or two, one blood or two?

Several theories have been put forward by ethnologists and archaeologists, but only one seems to me to provide a rational key to the characters both of the Highlander and the Lowlander, and that is the theory of two of the greatest of Celtic scholars, Dr Whitley Stokes and Professor Windisch. They hold the view that both Highlander and Lowlander are Celtic; that the one is Gaelic Celt, the other is Cymric Celt; that the Picts came to Britain from the Continent (Pict being the same word as Poitou) in an earlier wave of immigration than the Celts who were in occupation of Britain when Caesar came. In other words, the broad implication of this theory is that the basic race, both of the South and of the North of Scotland, is Celtic and that though the relationship between the two is that of cousinship and not of brotherhood, and that though the cousinship dates from many centuries BC, nevertheless fundamentally the land of Scotland is peopled by one blood.

The southern or Cymric Celt of Scotland always tended to face towards England, especially after the Roman walls went down and the fat lands of the *Pax Romana* lay open at last to hungry marauders, whereas the northern or Gaelic Celt always tended to face outwards to the islands, and, above all, to Ireland. As the centuries went on, the southern Celt was more and more exposed to the Norman and Saxon influences. The Gael on the other hand was perpetually being reinforced by the influx of Irish Gaels, always strengthening the blood and refurbishing the phoenix, and the tie between the two families of the Gael, who really were blood-brothers and not remote, prehistoric cousins, was knotted more closely than ever in AD 563 when Columba came from Ireland and landed upon the Holy Island of Iona.

Thus the southern and northern Celt drifted steadily further apart, until, after a thousand years or two, even the vague cousinship had been forgotten and the Highlander and Lowlander had become, in effect, two separate races with widely different characters. It is with these two characters that this book is concerned.

CHAPTER I

The Early History

In trying to make an estimate of the Highlander's character, it will be necessary to consider how he behaved when he came face to face with the most critical emergencies of his history during the last seven hundred years. Then, after we have obtained a rough, general sketch of his attitude to, and conduct in, times of stress, of danger, of difficult choice, of temptation, in times of victory and in times of defeat, it may be possible to draw some inferences about him and the manner of man that he has become in this twentieth century.

I have chosen the period of seven hundred years for two reasons. Firstly, because the Highlands have hardly any history at all during the long periods when they kept themselves to themselves. It is only when they come in contact with the outer world, a more civilised world where men can write down the happenings of the day, that they emerge from darkness. Here and there they emerge for a moment, into the golden light of the coming of Columba, into the legendary splendour of Kenneth MacAlpine, or into the glorious twilight of the endless wars against the Norsemen. But for the rest, the story is almost a complete blank until about the time of the millennium. The last of the Gaelic kings was driven from the throne by a combined army of Normans and Saxons in AD 1098, and thenceforward the infiltration of Southerners into the Lowlands was steady and irresistible. The Gael went back, mile by mile, towards the mountains, as the baronial armies and the feudal system pressed upon him, but he was not yet concentrated across the Highland Line in the fatal year when the great storm burst upon Scotland of which the thunder has never yet died away, of which the consequences have never been entirely reckoned, of which the damages have not been fully assessed, and for which, certainly, the bill has not yet been paid.

* * *

It is the purpose of this book, and indeed the sole reason for its existence at all, to prove that the critical date in the history of Scotland is 1292, the date on which Edward the First, King of England, examined the rival claims of the pretenders to the throne of Scotland and decided in favour of John Baliol. All the other important dates, the 1314 of Bannockburn, the 1513 of Flodden, the 1547 of Pinkie, the dates of the accession to the English throne of James the Sixth and First, of the Union of the Parliaments, of the rising of 1745, all are subsidiary to, and dependent on, the year in which John Baliol was handed the crown of Kenneth MacAlpine by a Frenchman from London. Before that time the relations between the two kingdoms had been, on the whole, in spite of such temporary set-backs as the Battle of Northallerton (the Standard) in 1138, cordial. The strong rule of William the First, the hatred with which the Saxons regarded the invader, and especially the devastation of the northern counties in 1070, drove numbers of Saxons across the border. Some Norman adventurers, who preferred an individual life to the rule of an iron king, also drifted to the north in the years after the Conquest, and the newcomers were welcomed by the Scottish king and, even more warmly perhaps, by his English Queen Margaret, sister of Edgar Atheling. After Margaret's death the Gaelic party tried to force the descendant of the hereditary Gaelic kings upon the throne of Scotland, but already the English and Norman influence was so strong that it was able to dethrone him and put in his place a southerner with the southern name of Edgar. He was followed by his younger brother David, the greatest of all kings of Scotland. David governed almost on the enlightened model of Alfred and under his rule the southern part of Scotland prospered materially and morally as it had never done before and did not do again for a long time.

Edgar and David were the first of England's contributions to Celtic Scotland. It was the only contribution which brought a benefit with it.

The period from 1124 to 1286 was certainly the first and, with the exception of the brief Renaissance flowering of the reign of James the Fourth, the only golden age in the history of the land. It was an era of peace, friendship with England, and wise statesmanship. The death of Alexander the Third in 1286, which brought an end to the golden age, plunged Scotland into the sequence of historical events which has been maintained to this day. Not for one moment has the sequence been upset or the chain of causation broken. Every link is in its place.

In 1296, ten years after Alexander's death, and one year after Baliol's forced accession, Edward, the Hammer of the Scots, made the first of his invasions. It is one of those strange coincidences, which are the despair of rationalists and the delight of poets, that the misfortunes of Scotland began in the very year in which the Celtic Stone of Destiny was taken away from Scone and placed by the Norman king in the Norman Abbey in Westminster. The theft of the sacred stone marked the beginning of centuries of bitterness and bloodshed.

In the first struggle for independence against the first and second Plantagenets the Gaelic clans played their part. The leader of the national rising was himself of Norman blood, of a family which had left Bruis, near Cherbourg, to follow the Conqueror and had worked its way north through estates in Yorkshire to estates in Annandale. But a considerable part of Bruce's army at Bannockburn was Gaelic.

But in the years after Bannockburn the Highlanders played a smaller and smaller part in the defence of the border. The Lord of the Isles and the Lord of Lorne might be all-powerful in their own lands, but it was Douglas and Randolph who held the gate against the English, and the great figures in Scottish history of the fourteenth century are not the chiefs of the Gaelic clans, but such heroes as the Knight of Liddesdale, Ramsay of Dalwolsy, and Black Agnes, the Countess of March. A strong king might have kept the clans within the rule of law, but after the death of Bruce a long minority, followed by three incompetent kings, enabled the clan chiefs to slip back into the primeval condition of independent patriarchy. Protected by their mountains and by their private armies of clansmen, the chiefs preferred savagery and self-government to the welfare of the country. So during the very years in which a fierce and burning patriotism was being kindled in the Lowlands, a cold isolation and parochialism was spreading through the glens. On the Border the great families, Cymric, Saxon, and Norman, united together for the defence of Scotland, while the great Gaelic families fought each other for a few yards of hill-side, or a mile or two of fishing-water, or a herd of cattle.

The Highlanders made one attempt, in the fifteenth century, to return to their old position in the government of the country. In 1411 Donald of the Isles made the last military throw of the dice of that historic and powerful lordship. He gathered his islesmen and mountaineers, MacDonalds, Macintoshes, Macleans, Macneills, and the rest, and marched across the Highland Line in the direction of Aberdeen, to re-establish the Gaelic domination and the Gaelic system of patriarchal local government.

If Donald had succeeded, Scotland might have been submerged for centuries. Just as the heavily armed infantry of Sparta dominated the whole of the Peloponnesus and throttled for hundreds of years almost all literary and artistic freedom of thought, so victory of the clansmen in 1411 would have stifled Scotland. But Donald, although he may have reckoned on meeting a new social order and a new military spirit engendered by the English wars, clearly had not understood that he would meet a new military tactic which had also come from the English wars. The army of lairds and burgesses and small gentry and citizens of Aberdeen had not only a stout body of infantrymen armed with the halberd. It also had a well-mounted body of cavalry on the Norman model. So long as the islesmen and the mountaineers remained on their own side of the Highland Line they had very little to fear from mounted men. But at Harlaw, in the open rolling country of Aberdeenshire, they were no match for horsemen, and the Lord of the Isles fell back to his own country, and the Lordship never again emerged as an independent fighting force.

The Battle of Harlaw was a symbol of the new policy which had been forced upon the Lowland gentry, the Ogilvies, Scrymgeours, and Irvines, and the other great families of the plains.

At Bannockburn the Highlanders and Lowlanders had stood shoulder to shoulder. But after the Highlanders had withdrawn from the common defence against the English and had decided to concentrate upon their own clan feuds in the mountains, the Lowland gentry was left to maintain the Border by itself. That it was undaunted by this task is proved by Harlaw. They made it perfectly clear on that battlefield that they had no intention of renewing the comradeship of Bannockburn and that they preferred to defend the Lowlands on two fronts, the northern as well as the southern, rather than risk an alliance with such a dubious ally as the Highlander.

The counter-attack of the Lowland Government after Harlaw was not long delayed, and the first strong King of the Central Government, James the First, defeated the islesmen and extinguished by forfeiture the Lordship of the Isles. The Battle of Harlaw was a decisive moment in the history of Scotland. The invasion of Donald was not a revival of the Gael in the sense that it was a national or racial uprising against the domination of the South. It was rather a personal attempt by a powerful chief to increase his personal possessions. Nevertheless, if it had succeeded it would have resulted in the over-running of many civilised counties by the clans. The Highland infantry only ventured across the Highland Line in an organised mass on four other occasions after Harlaw: under Montrose; on the excursion to Worcester with Charles the Second; and in 1715 and 1745. By their victory the Lowlanders not only emphasised the existence of the Highland Line, but they emphasised for the benefit of future generations the lesson which the Normans had taught to so many countries through so many scores of years, that a lightly armoured, semi-disciplined body of infantry, however brave, however aggressive, and however dexterous in the use of their weapons, could be no match for a steady body of infantry which had the assistance of heavily armoured horsemen.

Thenceforward the infantry of the clans was very chary of venturing into the comparatively flat country south and east of the Highland Line, where they were liable to be caught by veteran horsemen who had learnt their tactics in the English wars, or had ridden in the great charge which routed the cavalry of Henry the Fifth at the Bridge of Baugé.

The Highland clans therefore found themselves hemmed in behind their rampart of mountains, and their warlike activities were confined into two channels. They could either carry out hasty and undignified cattle-raids across the Line, the essence of which was to strike unexpectedly, and on the first sign of opposition to run for safety back into the mountains, or they could carry on local clan warfare between clan and clan, family and family. In this the Highland temperament excelled. It was a contest between man and man, with no horses on either side. Clan warfare was waged with deadly ferocity. Prisoners were almost always massacred, houses were always burned, and quarter neither given nor asked. These obscure battles are lost, perhaps fortunately, to history. Here and there a legend emerges, handed down from generation to generation in a poem or a piece of pipe music or in a bedtime story told by mothers to keep alive the spirit of hatred in their children. The classic case is the celebrated encounter on the North Inch of Perth between thirty champions of Clan Kay and thirty champions of Clan Chattan. It is worth mentioning the principal features of the battle because they throw a good deal of light upon the Highland character. In the first place there was a deadly hatred between the two clans; in the second, there was the reckless courage with which the sixty champions volunteered for the fray; thirdly, there was the sense of drama which chose the island in the middle of the Tay as the scene; and fourthly, there was the appearance of the Lowland mercenary who took the place of a defaulter of the Clan Chattan on payment of half a crown. Out of the sixty combatants only one has emerged from anonymity and that was the Lowlander, Henry Gow, the bandy-legged smith of Perth, who outfought the Highlanders with their own weapon in their own battle. This desire of enterprising and martial-minded Lowlanders to mingle in battle in the Highland ranks comes out over and over again in subsequent history and especially, as I will show later, in the World War of 1914-1918.

* * *

It is clear, therefore, that in spite of all his ferocity and skill in warfare, the Highlander, or Gaelic Celt, can only claim a small part of the credit of the maintenance of Scottish independence after Bannockburn. The right wing of the army at Flodden was composed of a medley crew of Highlanders commanded by the Earls of Argyll and Lennox. In all the list of the dead only Argyll himself and five others, Maclean of Duart, Mackenzie of Kintail, Stewart of Minto, and a Mackay and a Maclellan are of Highland name. And the men who fought at Otterburn were Douglases, Lindsays, Ramsays, Montgomerys, Hepburns, and Swintons; and at Homildon the only Highlanders were some Stewarts of Lorne, and at Halidon and Nevill's Cross and Pinkie there were no organised Gaels in the Scottish army.

The years went on and martial enthusiasm and physical prowess went on hacking away in the mountains. But gradually a new idea began to creep across the Line, an idea which was to cause the most vehement bitterness and animosity, and which was ultimately to bring the whole clan-system down in irremediable disaster. This new idea was simply that the law is, or ought to be, stronger than the sword. It was the idea which Rome had spread for the whole of the known world, but it had not penetrated north of the Roman wall, and when it ultimately began to creep westwards and northwards from Edinburgh, it caused the gravest consternation amongst the swordsmen. It required, of course, a strong central government, determined to support the law in the last necessity by force. A resolute lawyer in Edinburgh was only a match for a resolute soldier in the heather if he could count upon the ultimate support of a disciplined body of men-at-arms, but the moment he could so count upon such a body, the man in the heather was doomed.

One part of the Highlands proved its adaptability to the new idea with great success: the other part never understood it at all, and to this day feels that it was in some mysterious way the victim of some mysterious chicanery. It was the confederation of clans nearest to the south that grasped the importance of the new idea, and when the Clan Campbell had grasped it, they made the fullest possible use of it. The parchments, signed and sealed, came pouring across the hills from the Law Offices in Edinburgh, and the green tartan of the Campbells spread triumphantly in all directions, legally and all according to the book, while the red tartans of the less intelligent and less cultured clans further north, bewildered by this intangible and apparently omnipotent enemy, fell back sulkily further and further into the hills.

A new development followed logically. The parchments from the Law Offices depended upon the strength of the central government. Therefore the Clan Campbell had to be on good terms with the central government and had to follow it and support it on whatever course it might go. In the sixteenth century, that course suddenly took a violent and revolutionary turn and the Campbells had to turn with it. The Reformation had broken out in Europe, and England, the powerful kingdom of the Tudors, the victors on the disastrous field of Pinkie, had turned heretic. The Lowlands of Scotland followed suit. John Knox was let loose upon the Catholic faith and the Catholic churches, and Mary of Scotland was imprisoned by the heretical Elizabeth, and the heretical James, her son, reigned in Edinburgh.

The Campbells lost no time. They became as powerful a bulwark of Protestantism in Edinburgh as Edinburgh had been of the Campbell claims in the west. Each supported the other. Henceforth the Clan Diarmid fought their battles against the red tartan clans not only with legal documents, but with Calvin's bell, book, and candle as well, and again they triumphed over the Catholic clans of the north and west. The Highlands had always been divided into small clan sections. The Reformation divided them for the first time into two separate factions, the Protestant and the Catholic, and for the first time, the power of the central government in Edinburgh obtained through the Clan Campbell a permanent political footing west of the Highland Line.

In the seventeenth century the men of the sword gave two famous and utterly ineffectual demonstrations of the power of courage, determination, and cold steel, and the men of parchment replied with a stroke of which the echoes still reverberate round the world.

All the pent-up, baffled, sulky hatreds of the red tartan went with Montrose when he swept across the snowy passes into the heart of the Campbell country and captured Inneraora itself and destroyed for ever at Inverlochy the military power of MacCallum Mor, the chief of Clan Campbell. Personal bravery was an essential quality for a Highland chief if he was to lead his clan as a soldier, and when MacCallum Mor fled from Inverlochy in a galley he abdicated, on his own behalf and on behalf of his descendants, from the leadership of fighting men. But it made no difference to the prestige of the Marquises of Argyll. They still led their clan in intrigue, law-court, and council-chamber, and Montrose's head was not long in falling. For Montrose and the red tartans lived in the past. They were romantic and muddle-headed and childish. MacCallum Mor and the green tartans lived in the present. They were hard-headed and intelligent and grown-up. Montrose's cause was lost before it ever began, and not all the Dugald Dalgettys of Drumthwacket, not all the seventeenth-century Fluellens with their experience of the principles of the Lion of the North, could set it upon its feet.

Even more nebulous was Dundee's victory at Killiecrankie. Once again the Highland infantry swept everything before them in attack. But the leader was killed, and the victors went quietly home. In one wild moment the clansmen joined the famous armies of the world and then they walked back to the glens and did no more. The men of parchment went about affairs in a different way. They planned their work with decree and ordinance, and carried it out with writ and summons, and, above all, they did not move without the backing of London. This was one more logical development in their strategic system. Just as, in the first place, their documents were valueless without the support of Edinburgh, so now they added greater strength than ever to them by adding the support of London. Their stroke was to be no ephemeral affair. There was to be no quiet retreat after the victory. The work was to have a lasting effect. And it had. There is not one Scotsman in a hundred who can tell you a dozen details about the great march to Inverlochy or the great charge at Killiecrankie. You will find it difficult to discover a Scotsman who does not know something about the killing of the old men and the women and the children in Glencoe. When the swordsmen struck, the blows were dramatic and quite useless. When the Southerners struck, the blow was unheralded by shouts or by pibrochs, but it was deadly.

The feud in the Highlands between the red and the green grew in bitterness, if that were possible, after Glencoe, with the advantage always inclining towards the green.

CHAPTER II

The Rising of 1745 and the Campbells

Within a few years of the massacre of Glencoe, the Protestant clans found a new weapon.

The new Germano-Anglo-Swiss religion had helped them a great deal. The new German kings were to help them a great deal more. The Union of the Parliaments in 1707 transferred the political centre of Scotland to London, and the Campbells went south with it. The Camerons and Donalds wrapped themselves in a mist of vague anger and held fast to their ancestral clan-system. But it was too late. The world was going quickly past them and the key to Lochaber was moving from the Corrieairach to Whitehall. So it was only natural that when the north-western Highlands made their final attempts to impose an infantry-made king upon the ancient and peaceful country of England, the Clan Campbell came out strong and solid for German Geordie.

The history of those two attempts — especially of the Rising of 1745 — is one of the most valuable sources of illumination upon the Highland character. The Stuart Prince landed in Moidart with six companions to conquer the country which had, only a short thirty years before, smashed the power of the Grand Monarque at Ramillies and Oudenarde. He went to Glenfinnan and waited for the clans to come. Some came, some stayed away. Some sent the elder son to Glenfinnan and the younger to London. But the clans which came to the Raising of the Standard were the cream of the Highland attacking infantry. They swept Johnny Cope aside and they marched at extraordinary speed to Derby, and then they marched back. At times the army was animated by devotion to the Stuart dynasty, at others by a desire to take their loot home to the glens and stow it away in safety. And at Culloden one clan refused to fight because it was not given the right wing to defend which it had defended at Bannockburn. They claimed that it was their hereditary perquisite to defend the right wing of a Scottish army and they were careful to ignore their ancestors' conspicuous absence from Dupplin, Halidon, Homildon, Pinkie, and the rest of Scotland's battles against England. Probably Bannockburn was the only battle against England of which there was any tradition in the glens. Probably the rumours of the others had not reached them. At any rate, they maintained that the line of battle which had succeeded in 1314 ought to be reproduced in 1746. A sense of drama, a sense of fitness, and a passionate pride demanded it. Consideration of tactics, loyalty to the cause for which they had already sacrificed everything, and the ancestral joy of battle, were thrown to the winds. The tactics of Culloden were the usual Gaelic tactics, a strong charge and then brisk work with the sword. The only difference between Killiecrankie and Culloden was that the latter was a failure, and once the failure had set in, the Highlander would do no more. He was not a defensive soldier. He had not the qualities of the Saxon who fought at Hastings, or the ring of Lowlanders who surrounded the king at Flodden. He had no idea of fighting a rear-guard action in the style of Marshal Ney. With the Gael it was all or nothing. There must be either a smashing victory or else a smashing defeat.

So after the discipline and the artillery of Cumberland's Anglo-Scottish-German army had swept away the clans who tried to fight at Culloden, and the clan which refused, there was no defence of the Highland Line. The glens were open to the English and the Campbells and the Hessians.

It was the first time in history that the English, and their Teutonic cousins, had entered the glens, and they left their impress upon them, at first materially and a few months later, spiritually. The rising of 1745 and the march to Derby was one of the few occasions on which the English have been seriously frightened, and, as invariably has happened on these few occasions, the moment the cause for their fright was removed, the English flew into a violent rage. It was precisely the same after the Napoleonic wars, when the English Government despatched Sir Hudson Lowe to govern St Helena and inflict his long series of petty humiliations on the Emperor; it was the same instinct which made the ruling classes send the Tolpuddle martyrs to deportation out of sheer fright at the thought of united labour; it was the same instinct which blew sepoys from the guns and destroyed the old fort at Delhi after the Mutiny, imprisoned conscientious objectors during the World War of 1914-1918, and toyed for a moment with the idea of hanging the Kaiser.

After Culloden the instinct took the form of indiscriminate butchery, executions without trial, and the destruction of sheilings, houses, hamlets, and castles. The first time that the English crossed the Highland Line they did not see the beauty of the scenery or appreciate the possibilities of the trout-stream, the grouse-moor, or the deer-forest. The conditions of warfare sank back to the almost prehistoric era, before slavery became an institution, when prisoners of war were not even carried off to toil in mines or in galleys, but were simply killed at once. The Duke of Cumberland gave specific orders that no prisoners were to be taken. Out of this ignoble story of the flight and defeatism of one part of the Highlands, two comforts emerge for the descendants of the Jacobite clansmen, and out of the ignoble story of the cowardice and treachery of the other part of the Highlands, one comfort emerges for the descendants of the Whig clansmen. Take the Jacobite comforts first. Thirty thousand pounds in gold were offered as a reward for anyone who would give up Prince Charles Edward to the English, but no one came forward with the information and a claim. During the Prince's wanderings there were many men and women who could have earned the sum which was, at that time and in that wretched, devastated country, a fabulous fortune. But no one would do it. Clansmen had deserted Charles Edward in order to hide the loot from a battlefield in a safe place, or had refused to fight for him because their pride forbade it. But they would not sell him to the English. As we shall see from the later history of the Highlands, Prince Charles Edward was almost the only thing which the Highlanders did not sell to the English between 1746 and the present day. The second comfort is the loyalty of the broken clansmen to their chiefs.

After the fine careless enthusiasm for murder had a little abated in the breasts of the mixed Teutonic and Campbell invaders, the surviving rank and file of the defeated clans were no longer necessarily slaughtered on sight. They were often allowed to return to the ashes of their huts and the corpses of their less fortunate relations. The avenging angels, however, did not for a moment cease the pursuit of the chiefs who had rallied to the Royal Standard, and they succeeded in driving most of them into exile. The lands of the exiles were, of course, appropriated by the victors, or by the camp-followers who trailed cautiously behind the troops of the victors. To these new owners the clansmen, broken, harried, plunged into poverty, had to pay rent for their wretched plots of land. They also paid rent, a second rent, in some miraculous fashion, to the rightful patriarchs of the soil, the chiefs who had fled and were living in semi-starvation in France and the Low Countries. Loyalty to the chief was a far stronger instinct than loyalty to the Stuart king. And this was only natural. It was only a few hundred years ago that the Stuarts had been Stewarts, a clan like any other, and the line that had become royal had once been only patriarchal. So when the Standard was raised in Glenfinnan, the clans which rallied to it did so almost more because their chiefs demanded their loyalty than for the justice of the Royal cause, and when the enterprise had ended in universal calamity the memories of the survivors turned instinctively to their lost chiefs rather than to their lost Prince. These then are the two comforts which have been handed down by the simple

Jacobite clansmen to their descendants — indifference to blood-money and unswerving loyalty. The one comfort which has been handed down by the clans which clung to the German cause is that they chose the winning side.

* * *

This was a halycon time for the Clan Campbell. Their political cause and their religion had overwhelmingly triumphed and their influence was prodigious, not merely in Argyllshire and Edinburgh. It was powerful also in London. The memory of the unfortunate affair at Inverlochy was completely obliterated by the flood of legal documents, now no longer challenged or challengeable by the claymore, and Calvinism pushed Catholicism deeper than ever into the mountains and more remotely than ever into the islands. The classic example of the power of the Campbells after the rising of the Forty-five is the trial of James Stewart of the Glen for the murder of Colin Campbell, of Glenure, in 1752. That times had changed was very clear from the relationship of Glenure and Stewart, for Glenure was an Agent of the Crown on the forfeited estates of several Stewart gentlemen, and in the course of his work he had evicted James Stewart from his farm in Ardohiel in Appin. Fifty years before, or even twenty years before, the spectacle of a Campbell evicting an Appin Stewart from his farm without bloodshed and without resistance would have been rare. But the Highlands had changed and when Campbell of Glenure came to Stewart's farm, Stewart went out without a murmur. There was no evidence whatever that James Stewart had any hand in the murder of Glenure. Indeed he had everything to lose by it, and there was more than a suspicion that Alan Breck Stewart had done the deed. But from the Campbell point of view there was a profound difference between the two men, and the difference was simply this. They could not lay their hands upon Alan Breck, whereas they could, and did, lay their hands upon James. Up to this point the procedure had gone strictly in accordance with Highland tradition. A Campbell had been shot in Stewart country, and it served him right for being caught in Stewart country. A Stewart had been seized as a reprisal by the Campbells and taken to Inveraray, and it served him right for having committed the indiscretion of letting himself be caught. If the Campbells had hanged James Stewart there and then on no charge but simply that of being a Stewart on the day after a Campbell had been murdered, everything would have been in the best possible taste and in conformity with the best rules of Highland life.

But a new spirit was abroad and the Campbells acted in accordance with it, rather than the usage of the past. The rule of the sword was over and the rule of law, as practised in Edinburgh and enforced from London via Hanover, had taken its place. So James Stewart was charged with the murder of Glenure in the strictest legal form and tried in the strictest legal form before a judge and jury of his peers.

From the technical point of view, from the angle of the strictest legal correctitude, there was nothing wrong in the locality of the Court, which was that of the Hereditary Justiciar of Scotland, or in the presence of the Sheriff of Argyllshire on the Bench, or in the composition of the jury, or in the distribution of Counsel. It was just James Stewart's misfortune that the Court was in the town of Inveraray, the headquarters of the Clan Campbell, that the Hereditary Justiciar was the Duke of Argyll, the head of the Clan Campbell, that the Sheriff of the County was also the Duke of Argyll, that the fifteen jurymen happened to be all called Campbell, that the eight Counsel for the prosecution were led by the Lord Advocate himself from Edinburgh, and that the defence was in the hands of four obscure lawyers. The evidence legally brought forward by the legal experts consisted of two facts — that someone said that he had heard James Stewart say a year before the murder that he would go miles on his knees to kill the man who had evicted him from his farm in Ardshiel, and that on the day after the murder James Stewart had borrowed five guineas to give to Alan Breck who was leaving for France. On these two pieces of evidence James Stewart was hanged, and the Highlanders experienced their first taste of the new reign of law which had come to them from the south.

This famous trial marks a milestone in the history of the Highlands. The coming of the law of the State to supersede the law of the clan was the end of the old system. The two might have been combined in a compromise as in England where the administration of justice at Petty Sessions and even at Quarter Sessions has so often been a happy blend of state-law and paternal squirearchy. But to make such a blend of two systems workable, it is necessary that the men in charge of the administration should have an instinctive aptitude for compromise. The English squire has been for centuries an example of this aptitude and he has been, on the whole, an excellent magistrate. But it is very different in the Highlands where the idea of compromise was not well-known or well-liked. The abolition of the hereditary jurisdiction of the chiefs was accompanied by the abolition of the clan system of land tenure and the substitution of the proprietary system. In other words, the chief of the clan, if he had not been killed or exiled, after centuries of patriarchy and overlordship of the land on vague and customary rights was converted by an Act of Parliament, passed in London, into a laird with statutory title-deeds. When, therefore, the restoration of the estates forfeited by the chiefs who had gone out in the Forty-five took place in 1784, the chiefs or their descendants returned to a different status. They were no longer the first among equals, no longer the fathers of the glens. They were landowners established by the law and they owed their security and their rents and their rights not to their armed children, but to their factors and, above all, to their attorneys. They lost much by the change, but they also gained much, and the subsequent actions of a great many of them would seem to indicate that they did not regret what they had lost and that they were determined to make the fullest financial use of what they had gained.

* * *

But between the date of the Battle of Culloden and the Amnesty of 1784, two other events took place which must be chronicled. The first was the prohibition of the wearing of the Highland dress. That the infantry which had swept away the regular troops at Prestonpans and Falkirk, and had marched into the heart of England and terrified the good burghers of London, should be disarmed was an obvious and natural precaution against another rising. The Highlanders objected to the disarmament, but they did not resent it. It was a legitimate part of the military tradition to which they were accustomed. But the banning of the Highland dress was a different matter altogether. It was more subtle and more deadly, for it struck at one of the fundamental qualities of the Highland character. The origin of the dress is lost in the distant past and is the subject of conjecture and controversy. But whether the kilt began as a simple plaid, and whether the plaid began as an object of utility and not decoration, and whether the tartans were an early or medieval or even seventeenth-century invention, the important point is that by the middle of the eighteenth century the kilt had become incomparably the most picturesque male costume in Europe. The colouring was of endless variation, and all the accompaniments of lace, jewels, silver, steel, ebony, velvet, and in the case of the chief, of eagle's feathers, created an effect of elegance, splendour, and romance. To appreciate the force and subtlety of the prohibition it must be borne in mind that this costume was essentially the costume of the fighting men of the glens. It was a military costume and of course exclusively masculine. There are few sights so repugnant to the eyes of the Gael even today as a woman in a kilt.

When, therefore, the English took away the right to wear this splendid panoply of war they were striking at the very soul of the warrior. To disarm him of his long flint-lock gun, his claymore, and his dirk was nothing in comparison. He could always try to find a new equipment if he had not already hidden his old in the ground or in the thatch of his cottage. But when he had lost his kilt and his plaid he lost also the desire to find another gun and claymore, and dirk, and he no longer had the incentive to keep oiled and sharp the weapons in the ground or in the thatch. The clansmen could not go to battle in trousers. The miserable costume of the south was only fit for those who worked in fields and degraded themselves by manual labour, so the Highlanders lost their desire to fight, and put on the trousers of the Sassenach, and went to work in the fields.

Thus within a few years after the last armed eruption of the Gael into the affairs of Britain, the life of the Highlands had been radically changed. The military habit of life had gone, the military dress had gone, the clan system and the system of land tenure had gone, and a race which had maintained at least a semi-independence for a thousand years was brought into the political entity which centred in Whitehall. The only institution across the Highland Line which could not be entirely extirpated was the old religion. Not all the power of Calvinism backed as it was by the now triumphant Campbells could destroy the Catholicism of the seaboard clans or of the islands of the Hebrides. The second crucial happening between 1745 and 1784 is one of that long list of incalculable actions of the English which have made that incalculable race the bewilderment and the despair of foreign historians. Consider briefly the situation. The English had been frightened out of their wits; they had won the victory where at one moment they had expected to be utterly defeated; they had lost their tempers badly; they had behaved with savage ferocity to their conquered opponents. And then suddenly they turned round and produced one of their strange flashes of genius. It is this capacity for producing flashes of genius that is so bewildering. Why should a nation which is and always has been only faintly educated, produce the greatest list of poets since the days of Athens? Why should a nation which is probably in all apparent essentials the stupidest in Western Europe invariably succeed in any undertaking of any magnitude? Why should a nation which prides itself upon its placidity, its good-nature, and its sportsmanship lose its temper so badly when it is frightened, and commit such atrocities when the cause for fright has been removed? Why again should the same nation display an almost poetical insight into the characters of other nations when its bad temper has died down? It is probably true that the only people during many hundreds of years to whom the English, whether in success or in defeat, in good times or in bad, have never shown a real generosity are the Irish of the Catholic part of Ireland.

Wellington insisted that the Allies should treat France generously after 1815. The treaties of 1906 and 1907 which gave to the defeated Boers a large amount of self-government went a long way towards allaying the bitterness of the burning of the farms and the deaths of the women and children in the concentration camps. And after the war of 1914-1918 which gave the English one of the biggest frights which they have ever had, it was the English who maintained the post-war blockade of Germany, and thus killed many thousands of women and children from starvation, but when that fit of temper had passed, it was the English who devoted years to restoring Anglo-German friendship and preventing the French from trampling upon the defeated. Indeed, there is perhaps a significance in the fact that when the French, pursuing their trampling policy, invaded the Ruhr in 1923, the official British blessing on the enterprise should have been given not by an Englishman but by the Scots-Canadian, Bonar Law.

And so it was in their treatment of the Highlands. After 1750 the English began to recover their tempers. The Jacobite cause was irretrievably lost and the Hanoverian dynasty was firmly seated upon the Stone of Destiny in Westminster. The hour for generosity had come and the English seized it. They made a sweeping and magnificent gesture. They not merely allowed the broken barbarians of the mountains to return to their fancy dress and their coloured skirts, but they went even further. They allowed the Highlanders to resume their ancient profession of arms and gave them back their kilts and their guns simultaneously. There was only one trifling condition attached to the gesture and that was that the newly equipped and newly armed clansmen should be formed into regiments to fight side by side with the Anglo-German armies and not, as hitherto, against them. This stroke of genius is characteristic of the English blend of poetry and practical politics. The incomparable Highland infantry, if armed with English arms and trained and disciplined on the English model, would be more than a match for the French infantry in Europe or in India or the wide-open spaces of Canada.

Lowlanders had, of course, been tempted into the English service, both as individuals into English regiments and as a mass into organised Scottish regiments, nearly a century earlier and, even before the English stroke of poetical genius which invented Highland regiments, many individual Highlanders had enlisted in regiments of which the ultimate origin was London. John Graham of Claverhouse, for instance, had commanded the Royal Dragoons which had been raised for the express purpose of harrying the Covenanters who had "with great insolence flocked together frequently and openly in field conventicles, those rendezvouses of Rebellion"; in the original Lowland Royal Scots there was a company from Sutherlandshire; and although, in the original Black Watch, which was raised as a sort of gendarmerie in 1730, the colonel was the only officer who was not a member of the Whig-Calvinistic Clans of Campbell, Munro, and Grant, the rank and file had mainly drifted across the Line from Catholic and Jacobite clans into a more or less disciplined service.

But this was very different from the formation of the Highland regiments themselves. These new regiments were to be recruited in certain definite areas. Each was to march together as a unit. Each was to be officered by the men who were obviously destined to be officers by birth, marked out as officers by the clan-system, and selected as officers by the English.

It was the Anglicisation, on a new military model, of the fighting clan. Instead of recruiting these born soldiers in a haphazard way, and scattering them among a dozen different units, the English hit upon the idea of recruiting them into clan-regiments. Having destroyed the clans when they were hostile, England recreated the clan-system in her own service. For example, so long as the Camerons owed allegiance to Lochiel, London must destroy them. The moment the Clan Cameron was destroyed, and Lochiel exiled, and Achnacarry burnt, then London brilliantly invented the new Clan Cameron, and called it the Cameron Highlanders, a regiment of the English army. The vital difference, from the English point of view, was that the former had been an enemy, the latter became a servant.

But both enemy and servant were really only the same people, clansmen of Cameron of Lochiel.

This formation of the Highland regiments, which was the first time in history that the Gael allowed himself to be drilled in paraded Gaelic ranks to fight the battles of the Anglo-Saxon, was a sinister step towards the end of Gaeldom.

The destruction of the clan-system, with its land-customs, its law-customs, and its relationship-customs, was the beginning of that end. The formation of the regiments by taking away from the Highlands the prime of such youth as had been begotten by the survivors of the destruction, and the prime of such leaders as had avoided death at Carlisle or on Tower Hill hastened that end. The glens had been harried with fire and sword, and the flower of their fighting-men killed. Then, a short generation later, the glens were harried again with the King's shilling and recruiting-sergeant, and the flower of the men who could fight went away again. It makes small difference to the ultimate welfare of the glens that, in the first harrying, the clansmen fought in defence of the glens, and that in the second, they went abroad to fight for those who had harried the glens before.

It was all the same to the glens. They lost the flower, anyway.

But England gained, as England always does. Pitt, the Earl of Chatham, he who was inspired by the poetical genius of England to enlist the defeated Highlanders under the English flag, said in 1766:

"I sought for merit wherever it could be found, it is my boast that I was the first minister who looked for it, and found it, in the mountains of the north. I called it forth, and drew into your service a hardy and intrepid race of men — men who, when left by your jealousy, became a prey to the artifices of your enemies, and had gone nigh to have overturned the State, in the war before the last. These men in the last war were brought to combat on your side; they served with fidelity, as they fought with valour, and conquered for you in every quarter of the world."

That is one of the most magnificently statesman-like speeches in the English language. It is abounding with the inner, wise spirit of England. It is also startlingly frank.

CHAPTER III

The Highland Clearances

It did not take long for the Chiefs who had had their status altered from patriarchy to lairdship to discover the financial possibilities of their new position. The rents which came in from the farms and small-holdings were small enough and were often in arrears, and when a new idea began to filter northwards by which money would be more easily come by, the new lairds applied. themselves to it with eagerness.

The new idea was, of course, that wool was in great demand and that wool came from sheep. The Chiefs owned the land on which sheep could graze and the only obstacle which stood between them and the establishment of large and profitable sheep farms was the presence on the land of the clansmen. But the clansmen held their crofts on very short leases and the Chiefs found no difficulty in applying the processes of the law and in evicting by the sharpness of their attorneys the men who had held the land for centuries by the sharpness of their swords. The loyalty of the men who went to Glenfinnan, who would not betray the Prince for £30,000, who squeezed the second rent out of the ruined farms to support the exiled patriarchs, was all forgotten as if it had never existed, and the men were driven off the land and the sheep took their place. What happened to the men?

Some enlisted in the new Highland regiments. Many thousands emigrated unhappily to Canada. These lost their native land for ever and endured toil and danger and sorrow. Many died on the voyage, for the conditions on the emigrant ships were horrible and no provision had been made for medical emergencies, and many died in the early struggles to found the new settlements. But the survivors were the happiest in the end. They created a new life for themselves, a life that was free and therefore dignified.

But those who stayed behind were soon faced with a dreadful choice, whether to stay in the glens, now being run on the new pastoral-profit system, or whether to try their luck in the new industrial city of Glasgow. At first these survivors of the old patriarchy held doggedly to their huddled and overcrowded townships and counted themselves lucky that they were not singing "By the waters of the Fraser River we sat down and wept." But soon they were weeping by the waters of the Clyde. All the best land was taken for the sheep. Barren patches were given to some of the men and the rest were driven down to new townships on the seashore and forcibly converted from farmers to fishermen. There was not even a living to be got, let alone a livelihood, and starvation, or semi-starvation, began to drive them down to the machines in Glasgow. They might as well have stayed among the juniper and the larches and the heather, and far better have gone to the Fraser River, for they were as near starvation in Glasgow as ever they were upon the moor of Rannoch.

The machines were a new life to the Lowlander; to the Highlander they were death. His paradoxical mixture of pugnacity and defeatism, his surface amiability, and his incapacity to adapt himself quickly to the changes in a new world, and his defeatism, quickly became his dominant instincts. Again he could not fight a defensive action. He simply went to the wall.

It is very seldom that I find myself in disagreement with my friend and compatriot, Mr Moray McLaren, in anything he writes. But I cannot agree with his conclusion in his *Return to Scotland* that "the same romanticism that had built the Celtic character in those moors had enabled them to believe in the great romantic fraud of Industrialism."

If I read Mr McLaren correctly in this sentence he would seem to imply that it was a spirit of adventure which sent the clansmen south to Glasgow, and that they set out from the glens in search of romance, and found it. I simply do not believe it. They were driven into Glasgow by the semi-starvation which was caused by the Clearances. They no more wanted to exchange the hill-sides for the slums than the emigrants wanted to exchange Lochaber for the unknown NorthWest.

Both were forced against their will and I believe that the Gaelic character is not so constructed that it would be deceived by a bogus romanticism. It is true that the Highlander has romantic ideas about certain things, but most emphatically they are not the things about which he is popularly supposed to be romantic. He did not march to the Raising of the Standard at Glenfinnan because it was romantic but because he thought it was right, and he went into Glasgow for the utilitarian purpose of feeding himself, and not because he saw beauty in slag-heaps or visions in the smoke of factory chimneys.

No man who had lived under the same sky as the golden eagle or had seen the reflection of the osprey in the waters of Loch-an-Eilan would willingly, of his accord, have gone to live in the Cowcaddens.

But one thing is certain. Whether the clansmen emigrated or enlisted or went to Glasgow or stayed in the glens, it was "Lochaber No More" for all of them. The old days were finished.

* * *

The most famous of the Clearances were those on the estates of the Sutherland family. The heiress of the Sutherlands had married a young Englishman, Leveson-Gower, the Marquess of Stafford, and it was he who hit upon the device of converting the greater part of Sutherlandshire into a sheep farm. It may be excused to him that he was an Englishman who did not know and did not recognise clan loyalty and also that he spent many thousands of pounds on the improvement of roads and bridges in the county, but that excuse cannot be put forward for the Chiefs of the Jacobite clans who threw themselves so eagerly into the new get-rich-quick idea.

* * *

At first the new experiment was a great success. The sheep were even more docile than the men had been, and the increasing spread of the industrial revolution, particularly in the Ridings of Yorkshire, created a great demand for wool. The machines were being invented for Bradford and Huddersfield, and the Highland lairds had no reason to regret the commercial aspect, at least, of their latest contribution to the welfare and amenities of their glens. But nothing remains static, especially where the English are concerned, and as the demand for wool increased by leaps and bounds so did the organisation of the English wool-spinners spread its tentacles over the world. Australia soon came into the field with a mass-production of wool, more cheaply and more efficiently than the comparatively small flocks of Scotland. So the sheep industry in the north began to decline, and it was poor consolation to the lairds who saw their revenues shrinking year by year, to know that a great part of the Australian competition was in the hands of clansmen who had been evicted years before. But whatever the effect of the new production of wool in Australia might have upon the glens, it was very satisfactory to the English who acquired at one and the same time wool for Yorkshire, a market for Birmingham, and another sentimental link in the far-flung chain of Empire.

But the lairds who had once been the Chiefs did not propose to sink back into financial straits again. They had tasted once the joys of easy money and they looked round for a new method of recapturing those joys. The first time it was sheep, the second time it was deer. In the 1870's and 1880's they began to evict the sheep, and just as they had once turned agricultural land into pasture so they now began to turn the pasture-land into forests.

Kipling has a story called *Letting in the Jungle*, in which Hathi, the elephant, called in his brothers and destroyed the village which had ill-treated Mowgli.

The lairds were as systematic and as efficient, though not nearly so intelligent, as the elephants. They let in the jungle across the north and west of Scotland, and once again they drove the survivors of the clans into small huddled townships to starve or to emigrate or to fish, whichever they pleased. The conditions of these survivors were desperate, so desperate indeed that rumours began to filter slowly southwards that all was not well in the Highlands. There was a great barrier of inertia, and an even greater barrier of powerful vested interest, to prevent these rumours from reaching Whitehall, and it is a strong proof of the appalling state of affairs that they did at last penetrate and that an official Commission into the conditions of the cottars and crofters of the Highlands and Islands was set up. The Commission travelled extensively in the afflicted districts and took evidence from hundreds of witnesses. Their conclusions were published in four large volumes in 1884, and these verbatim reports of the evidence that was given are a damning indictment of the Chiefs of the clans.

In those four volumes, long ago forgotten upon dusty shelves in a government department and a few official libraries, can be found the whole miserable story, told in words of dignity and restraint by the men who had suffered. Their answers are given verbatim, and the cadences and turn of the phrases strike the ear.

As William Power has said in *Literature and Oatmeal*:

"One of the real reasons for this fine diction is that the people in these districts learned English from priests, ministers, landlords, and chiefs. Their English is not a patois; it is the English of gentlemen and scholars. The other real reason is bilingualism. Their native culture is Gaelic, and much of their English represents an attempted translation from an older and finer tongue."

I am going to quote a few of these verbatim replies, and the reader must remember that the men who made these replies to the Government's commission were often the poorest and humblest farm labourers or fishermen, poorer by far than any man in the corresponding walk in England. I doubt if the rustic hinds of Gloucestershire or Worcestershire, settled for centuries in a plump and sleek countryside, would have spoken so well as this struggling peasantry.

The same story runs through all the answers of the witnesses, a story of eviction, of over-crowding into narrow spaces to make way for the trees of absentee proprietors, of innumerable restrictions and penalties, and of the hopelessness of trying to seek redress. It is a story told by men whose eyes are always turned to the past, never to the future.

Angus Stewart, of Skye, said that there were twenty-six tenants on the Braes of Beinn-a-Chorrain where in his grandfather's day there were five. The new tenants had been cleared off the deer-forest.

Question: "When the land was subdivided among these new crofters, who built the houses?"

Stewart: "The poor crofters themselves."

Question: "Did they get any assistance in building them?"

Stewart: "May the Lord look upon you! I have seen myself compelled to go to the deer-forest to steal thatch — to steal the wherewithal to thatch our houses. If we had not done so, we should have had none."

John Nelson, also of Skye, said:

"We have hill pasture, but we are only allowed to graze a cow upon it, and we are allowed to keep a cat, but we are forbidden to keep dogs. The hill pasture is not a day without from 100 to 200 sheep grazing upon it, and we are ourselves not allowed to graze a herd of sheep upon it. Two or three years ago the only sheep in our townships was one that was a pet."

Donald M'Kinnon, Skye, said:

"We have forty-five families in Elgoll in a township about a mile square, and besides these there are seventeen other families in our midst. There is beside us a township, Keppoch, from which forty-four families were removed, and sixteen of them were sent away to Australia."

Question: "Who is your proprietor?"

M'Kinnon: "Mr Alexander Macallister."

Question: "Does he stay on the property?"

M'Kinnon: "No."

Question: "Do you recollect any resident proprietor?"

M'Kinnon: "Not in my recollection."

Question: "Have you ever seen your proprietor?"

M'Kinnon: "Yes. About forty years ago."

Hector Macpherson, of Harrapool, said:

"There are game and rabbits on our grazing. They are very troublesome."

Question: "Are you not aware that you can protect yourselves now to some extent?"

Macpherson: "No, because we are tenants at will. We cannot protect ourselves. There is no fixity of tenure."

Question: "Don't you even try to trap them?"

Macpherson: "No, we don't even dare to trap them. If we did we might be put in jail — if there was room for us."

Over and over again echoes of earlier clearances and unforgotten tragedies break through, either from old men who saw them or younger men who knew of them by hearsay.

Donald M'Innes, seventy-five years of age, remembered very well the evictions from Boreraig.

"One man perished. It was in the time of snow when they were evicted. The man was found dead at his own door after he had been evicted. Their fires were extinguished and their houses knocked down, and themselves put out much against their will — the officers compelling them."

Donald M'Leod, seventy-eight years old, a crofter of Kyle-Rona, did not remember the very first evictions on Rona which began in the time of M'Leod himself about forty years before, but he well remembered Mr Rainy — thirty years before — clearing fourteen townships to make a sheep-farm.

"The people went to other kingdoms — some to America, some to Australia, and other places that they could think of. Mr Rainy enacted a rule that no one should marry in the Island. There was one man who married in spite of him, and because he did so, he put him out of his father's house, and that man went to a bothy — to a sheep-cot. Mr Rainy then came and demolished the sheep-cot upon him, and extinguished his fire, and neither friend nor anyone else dared give him a night's shelter. He was not allowed entrance into any house. His name was John M'Leod. There were hundreds, young and old, in the two townships. The land was altogether arable land capable of being ploughed. The only occupants of that land today are rabbits and deer and sheep."

Alexander M'Lennan, seventy-four, said:

"I was at the ships when the people were sent off, and they were like lambs separated from their mothers. There was one old man there who said, 'Should I go to Australia I may die on my arrival. I should prefer remaining in Raasay, but I must go.'"

Angus Sutherland (Sutherlandshire) knew of the earlier clearances by hearsay.

He said:

"In the year 1815 when many natives of the parish were fighting for their country at Waterloo, their houses were being burned in Kildonan Strath by those who had the management of the Sutherland estate . . . the entire population of close on 2000, who had previously divided 133,000 acres of land, were compressed into a space of about 3000 acres of the most barren and sterile land in the parish: and the remaining 130,000 acres were divided among six sheep farmers. . . ."

Of conditions in Sutherlandshire as he knew them from experience, Angus Sutherland said:

"In winter we have to resort to whins or furze to keep our cattle alive. This is braised or pounded with a flail, and then given to the cattle. When that fails, we must use seaweed to feed them with."

Duncan M'Kinnon, from Tiree, said:

"My father and grandfather occupied the croft from time immemorial, yet were evicted for sheep. My father was about seventy-five years of age when we were evicted."

The Rev. Roderick Morison, minister for the third generation in the parish of Kintail, said:

"It is possible to walk from within a mile of Beauly station to the Cro of Kintail without putting a foot on anything but deer forest, practically from sea to sea; the whole north side of Glen Affric is a vast deer forest extending also to the Cro of Kintail; from Invergarry House you can walk on forest land all the way down to the sea at Knoydart." . . .

But Mr Morison's catalogue is too long to give in full. The whole land was covered with trees. Colin Chisholm (aged 72), retired Custom House officer, said:

"The whole of Glencannich (14 miles in length and averaging about 3 in breadth), except one small farm, is at present a deer forest. But in my early recollection there were 33 tenant farmers residing in Glencannich. There were also 12 families of cottars. In my own time there were 17 Glencannich men who held commissions in His Majesty's army; there were also 9 Glencannich men in Holy Orders; they were clergymen in the Catholic Church."

"Later on," he went on, "Strathglass was cleared and the farms were let to strangers. Lord Lovat ('the humane Lord Lovat') gave the evicted tenants farms in Glenstrathfarrar. Glenstrathfarrar also was a nursery of brave soldiers who distinguished themselves under their chief General Fraser, on the Heights of Abraham. In 1855 there were 22 families on the estate of Guisachan. But Lord Tweedmouth [at that date Mr Marjoribanks] bought it saying — 'the scenery is very fine; but it was the game that induced me to purchase it' — and evicted them all."

Mr Marjoribanks was only one of the great English invasion, and he, like the Marquess of Stafford who afterwards became the Duke of Sutherland, stoutly denied that he had done harm to his estate, or indeed had done anything except good. He gave evidence before the Commission and described the improvements which he had carried out, at his own expense.

It was true, he said, that all the tenants on Guisachan had gone, but he had not evicted them. More than that, he advanced a positive theory as well as his own negatives.

"The Highland Railway has caused a greater amount of depopulation in the glens than all the other causes of the last 50 years."

Sir John Ramsden had been perhaps the most lavish of all in his expenditure, but he did not claim that his whole outlay had been for the direct benefit of the community. He had spent altogether about £180,000 on his estate at Ardverikie (near Ben Alder where Cluny Macpherson hid for years after the '45), and Alvie, on Speyside, and a part of that money was spent on houses for gillies and lodges for keepers. But there are two items in Sir John Ramsden's expenditure which in themselves explain and illuminate the whole campaign for the letting in of the jungle and the keeping out of the human beings. The first item is "one hundred miles of fencing," and the second is "twenty-four million trees."

"I have planted," said Sir John, giving evidence, "eight thousand acres at Ardverikie and Alvie with twenty-four million trees. I am going to plant from my tree-nursery two million trees each year in future."

But there was another side, even to Sir John Ramsden's munificent benefactions.

The Rev. Evan Gordon, minister of a Gaelic Church in Glasgow, was asked by the Commissioners:

"Do you think, in spite of the £200,000 that has been spent by Sir John Ramsden in twelve years, the people are poorer than when Sir John went there?"

Mr Gordon replied: "I don't at all maintain that they are more impoverished, but the people are not there. That is the point."

Question: "But if the land, when Sir John went there, was occupied by the same number of people, how can there be fewer people now?"

Mr Gordon: "What I maintain is that the people are not there as I have seen them."

Question: "But were they there when Sir John went there?"

Mr Gordon: "Most decidedly, and many of them even after the Marquis of Abercorn got the lease and turned it into forest."

Question: "But the £200,000 was spent by Sir John after the people had disappeared?"

Mr Gordon: "Precisely."

Question: "There was a removal from there (Alvie), but it could hardly be called an eviction?"

Mr Gordon: "No, they were put down just on the banks of the Spey, and planted down on one of the poorest pieces of land you could get anywhere, and the people had to trench the ground. No doubt Sir John had planted a great many trees, and that is a very valuable product of the soil, but then the people were deprived of what they had."

But the Marjoribanks's and the Ramsdens, with their wire fences and their tree-nurseries, were not the deadliest captains of the invading armies of sportsmen. While the industrial revolution in England had been quickly creating a new class of nabob, the expansion and development of the United States of America had been doing the same thing at a prodigious rate, and the products of the American process were not always very pleasing citizens. One of these was a Mr Winans.

Mr Winans came to Scotland and determined to be in the vogue and create for himself a deer-forest. He soon found a Chief who would sell him the land without any tiresome legal clauses restricting the purchasers' right to evict sitting tenants, and in due time Mr Winans became a Highland sportsman.

Colin Chisholm, the old exciseman, had something to say about Mr Winans to the Commission of Enquiry.

Colin Chisholm: "We read in the public prints that an American, Mr Winans, has turned nearly 250,000 acres in the counties of Ross and Inverness into a deer-forest. I go occasionally to the west coast, and wend my way through Glencannich. From the road I see the heavy crop of natural grass waving on the hill-side and meadows, half-tame deer browsing at ease among crumbled walls; empty but substantial houses — some slated and some thatched, still standing at intervals in the glen, their windows bolted and their doors locked up."

Question: "Who are the proprietors who have cleared their land and made it forest for Mr Winans?"

Colin Chisholm: "First and foremost — Mackenzie of Kintail."

Question: "Mr Winan's style of doing the thing is very different?"

Colin Chisholm: "Ach, I don't like his butchering style of killing game at all."

Question: "What is his style?"

Colin Chisholm: "Gathering the poor animals together and driving them before the muzzles of the guns."

Question: "Does he not stalk them?"

Colin Chisholm: "You might as well send an elephant after them to stalk them."

Another landowner of the district, a Mr Duncan Darroch, praised the efforts of Mackenzie of Kintail to prevent the Winans evictions, but he did not defend, nor could anyone defend, Kintail's original action in selling the tenants without a safeguard.

On an island near Tobermory, the proprietor — a Mr Clark — closed up with stones the only good well, and so cleared the island entirely of its numerous inhabitants.

The Commissioners of Enquiry had two favourite subjects to which they returned incessantly, the Army and Emigration. Nor can they be blamed for it. From time immemorial, in many other countries besides Scotland, those in authority have been accustomed to put forward these two sovereign remedies for poverty and under-nourishment. "Enlist or Get Out" has enjoyed wide and long popularity as a constructive governmental slogan.

Donald M'Neill, of Skye, was asked:

"Do many people in Skye enlist in the army?"

M'Neill: "Very few indeed."

Question: "Why don't they enlist now?"

M'Neill: "Because they are impoverished and sunk down, without any spirit of enterprise whatever. Why should we fight for our Kingdom when we see so much poverty and neglect by our sovereign and legislators?"

The spirit had indeed changed since the days when Chatham raised the regiments. Yet the men who enlisted eagerly in those regiments were men whose families had been broken in battle and in persecution, whose lands had been taken, and whose memories were memories of killings and burnings and starvings. But the vital, the essential, difference was that the men of 1750 had suffered at the hands of the alien and that need break no man's spirit. The men of 1880 were suffering at the hands of their own blood, and that would break any man's.

John Campbell, crofter's son and soldier, said:

"From Dervaig (Tobermory) in the time of the Crimean war there were seven of us in Her Majesty's service, and four of us went up the Alma, and I am the most insignificant of the whole. We went through the whole of the Crimean war. Three of us again went through the whole of the Indian Mutiny. In Afghanistan we were represented by one of our number, Allan Macdonald, who was killed at the last battle of Candahar. We have fourteen war-medals, a star, and twenty-one clasps in our village."

Question: "But notwithstanding all these services you have been ill-used in the matter of your possessions?"

John Campbell: "We complain bitterly that we cannot get these houses which our forefathers paid for."

Question: "Is there any difficulty in recruiting men for the army?"

John Campbell: "No, but there are no men in our parish — nothing but sheep and game. There were four Waterloo men in the parish. They came home and told stories, and the young men would be delighted to be connected with the army. But the army is less popular now. The people are crushed down now. All their life is crushed out of them."

John Nicolson, of Rona, was asked why he did not emigrate as so many of his friends had done. He said:

"There are more of my friends in America and Australia than there are in Raasay, and I have not seen or heard my father or mother got a paper or a letter asking them to go out there, and I am not aware that a pound note or a shilling ever came to them to help them, to show that that land was better than the place they had left. It is likely that I would rather stay in Rona, bad as it is, than try my chance in these places. I am there for some time past at any rate, and I am trying sea and land, and everyone in the place is in the same way."

Donald Nicholson described how he was evicted at the age of seventy-three. His rent had been suddenly doubled, which he had accepted, and then another £1 added, which he had refused to pay. These are his own simple and moving words:

> "When the summer came the officer came and ejected me. He put everything I had out of the house, and I was only wanting payment for my houses, and I would go. The doors were locked on me. The tacksman of Monkstadt sent word round to the rest of the crofters that anyone who would open door for me would be treated the same way as I was next year — and they are here today — and not one of them would let me into his house, they were so afraid. I could not cut a peat. My son's wife was in with her two young children, and we that night in the cart-shed, and our neighbours were afraid to let us in, and crying over us. The peats were locked up. They still had the mark upon us. We had not a fire to prepare a cake. There was plenty of meal outside, but we had not a fire to prepare it. I was then staying in the stable during the summer. I could only make one bed in it. My daughter and my son's wife and the two children were sleeping in that bed, and I myself was sleeping on the stones."

It was not only the new get-rich-quick landlordism which the crofters had to face. There was the steady growth of Calvinism as well, creeping and blighting and deadening.

John M'Lean, a seventy-three-year-old crofter of Waternish, in Skye, was asked:

> "When you were young had the people more amusements and diversions than they have now?"
>
> He replied: "Yes, much more."
>
> Question: "What sort of diversions?"
>
> John M'Lean: "Balls and dances at some times of the year — at Christmas. They don't have such now."
>
> Question: "Had they more music?"
>
> John M'Lean: "Yes."
>
> Question: "What sort of music?"
>
> John M'Lean: "Pipe. We don't hear the pipe at all in the place now."
>
> Question: "Did they sing more?"
>
> John M'Lean: "Yes, plenty of songs."
>
> Question: "Men and women?"
>
> John M'Lean: "Yes."
>
> Question: "What has made them less cheerful? Have the clergy discountenanced those amusements, or is it the deterioration of their condition?"

John M'Lean: "The ministers were, of course, discountenancing it. The ministers won't be for the like of that at all."

Or take the evidence of Alexander Mackenzie, of Boreraig in Skye; he was asked:

"Was your town famous of old as the seat of the pipers of Skye?"
Alexander Mackenzie: "Yes, the M'Crimmons had the township as the hereditary pipers of the M'Leods."
Question: "How long is it since the last of M'Crimmons?"
Alexander Mackenzie: "I cannot tell, but my grandfather came to the place when it was first settled, and that was over eighty years ago."
Question: "Is there any music now among the people?"
Alexander Mackenzie: "No."
Question: "Is there not one piper in all Duirinish?"
Alexander Mackenzie: "No."
Question: "You have explained all about the fishing in a very intelligible way. Will you give an explanation how the pipe music has so much gone out in Skye?"
Alexander Mackenzie: "My opinion is that in those days of pipe music they were looking more to the Pope than they are today, and I believe it is the gospel that has done away with the pipe. It was death that did away with the M'Crimmons."

Then come two terrible answers, in which all the tragedy of the Highlands is compressed.

Question: "Are you fond of music yourself?"
Alexander Mackenzie: "I don't care should I not hear music any day of the year, if I was well off in other ways."
Question: "If you were well off would not music and dancing come back again?"
Alexander Mackenzie: "No doubt it would leave us happier, but I don't know whether it would set us to dance or no."

The same thread runs through all the story. Everyone is looking back to the past, when there was land for all and a chance to live, and a life to be gay about. John Bethune said that forty and fifty years before the women were not obliged to draw the harrows in Beruisdale or work in the fields; he remembered the time when there were twenty horses in Beruisdale, but now the landlords forbid them to be kept.

John Mackenzie said: "I can say with truth that the people were better off in my young days than they are now. They were shod and clothed better. The whole district was entirely deprived, of hill pasture, and our stock are crowded in so that they are spoiled. Unless we get the rent reduced to a sober rent, we cannot hold up to it long. We will soon lose all we have. Our stock has got reduced, and our money has gone."

Then come two very singular sentences in John Mackenzie's evidence:

"We were hearing of good news from Ireland. We were much inclined to turn rebels ourselves in order to obtain the same benefits."

But the days of Highland rebellions were over.

I will end this sad story with two quotations, also from the evidence given to the Commission, about the manner of men who were thus driven from the straths of their forefathers.

Aeneas Ranald Macdonell, an advocate in Morar in Inverness-shire, a man of sixty, said:

"From the recollection of the people long ago in my boyhood, I should say that the old people were a finer race; I mean the fathers and grandfathers of these here. They were fine-looking men, and men of an independent noble spirit, who were on the most cordial and friendly terms with their chiefs. At that time it was Clanranald, and I have no doubt it was the same with Lochiel's people. They looked upon the Chief as their father, and had no fear or awe such as they have of proprietors nowadays."

And when Mr Gordon was asked: "I suppose the importance of the Comyns of Badenoch consisted very much in the number of men who were upon their possessions?"

He replied:

"Decidedly. If it will be agreeable to the Commission, I will state a very interesting fact with regard to the last Duke of Gordon. The last time he paid a visit to the country, shortly after he sold it, they mustered the clans. They came down from the Lochaber country, and Cluny Macpherson and other chiefs led the men, and they were all dressed in the Highland garb and armed and placed in array on a piece of elevated ground on the east side of Kingussie. When the Duke appeared in his carriage and four, he was received by some of the officers, and he looked at the men, and I can assure you he wept bitterly, and said, 'If yesterday had been today, neither Badenoch nor any property in Lochaber would have been sold. I have never seen such a body of men.' Well, the most of these melted away after the Duke sold the property, and they are to be found now in every quarter of the globe."

* * *

It may be that I have devoted too much attention to the second clearances for the deer, and too little to the first, for the sheep. The first set the evil precedent; they were at least fifty years nearer to the great loyalties of the '45 and after; and they evicted a great many more people. But although they were inspired by the new English ideas of finance and industry, and although the most celebrated example was the English Marquess of Stafford's, yet, in the main, the sheep-clearances were carried out by Scotsmen for their own pockets and, in the main, the pastures remained in Scottish ownership.

The clearances for the deer were different. They were inspired by the Englishman's ideas of sport. There was no pretence that the new forests would be of material benefit to the whole community. There was no hypocrisy about it. The industrial revolution in England was by this time working through its third or fourth generation of dynastic cotton-spinners, wool-weavers, coal-owners, bankers, shippers, and all the thousand money-making professions of the Victorian era, and a wealthy class had been created which could rest upon the golden laurels of its fathers, grandfathers, and great-grandfathers, and enjoy a leisure which a great many of them had not earned. It was for these that the deer-forests were created. These men had vast riches, and all the Englishman's hereditary love of sport, and it was for them that the last of the Chiefs sacrificed the last of their clansmen. At the date of the publication of the Report into the conditions of the crofters and cottars (1884), the names and acreage of thirty-seven deer-forests are recorded for the county of Inverness. Thirty-one of them were at that time occupied, that is to say either owned or rented, by gentlemen with Anglo-Saxon names. Forty-four deer-forests are recorded for the county of Ross and Cromarty. Thirty-seven were owned or rented by gentlemen with Anglo-Saxon names.

The first clearances, then, were for the benefit of Scots who saw an advantage in the adaptation of their lives and surroundings to an English economic idea. The second were for the benefit of Scots who saw an advantage in the importation of an English social idea. In the first, only the idea came north; in the second, the English came too. It was their second invasion of the glens in history, and, by an odd coincidence, they invaded with the same sort of allies as on the first. In 1746 they came with Hessian and Hanoverian friends; in the 1870's and 1880's they had colleagues from Frankfort and Amsterdam. On both occasions they came to shoot. But there were some differences between the two invasions: on the first the English did most of their own burning and starving and evicting. And on the first, though they forbade the Highlander to wear the kilt, they did not wear it themselves. And on the first, after they had ruined the country, at least they went away.

CHAPTER IV

The 51st Highland and the 52nd Lowland

On the outbreak of the World War, the Highlands made four notable contributions to the Allied cause. There was, first, the handful of men who came from the depopulated glens.

Secondly, there were the Canadian Highlanders, descendants of the men who had gone out to fight under Wolfe, or who had been driven out to make room for the sheep and the deer. The blood was still strong, the heart was Highland, and the memories of the Clearances had faded, and they came back to fight for the country which had discarded their fathers.

The third was the fisher-folk who went mine-sweeping. The fourth contribution to the Allied cause was far more important that the other three, and, as it sprang from the essential roots of the Highland character and its influence upon the world, it must be examined with care. If the story of the 51st Highland Division of the Territorial Force during the war of 1914- 1918 is appreciated and properly understood, it will be found to contain in itself a complete miniature of all that I am trying to elucidate.

In addition to the regular battalions of the Scottish regiments in the pre-war British army, two new divisions were raised in Scotland after the outbreak of the war, numbered respectively the 9th and 15th, and the two territorial divisions, the 51st Highland and the 52nd Lowland, were mobilised on August 3rd, 1914. Scotland also contributed a number of separate units, yeomanry, garrison artillery, mountain-artillery, and so on, and regiments of Scotsmen were recruited in England, such as the London Scottish, Liverpool Scottish, and Tyneside Scottish.

The 9th, 15th, and 51st went out to France or Flanders at approximately the same time, the spring of 1915, and the 52nd went eastwards. At the beginning it appeared that the 9th and the 15th held an advantage in many ways over the 51st. Both were units of Lord Kitchener's army, and therefore received preferential treatment from that muddle-headed and obstinate man who disliked the territorial army mainly because he had not been concerned in its formation. In addition to that advantage the 9th Division had been widely publicised by Mr Ian Hay in his book *The First Hundred Thousand*. Later in 1915, when the 9th and 15th Divisions had performed exploits of wonderful bravery at Loos and Hulluch, in that battle which was so badly managed by the High Command that it made Neuve Chapelle seem almost a well-conducted battle, Mr Ian Hay again unlimbered his skilful pen, and wrote a fine description of the exploits of the Scottish troops. On the other hand, the 51st Division, which had been thrown against uncut barbed wire at Festubert by the regular officers who were already, as early as May, 1915, crowding into every available staff appointment, and although it had fought as bravely at Festubert as the 9th and 15th at Loos, there was no Ian Hay to write their story. In 1916, at the Battle of the Somme, the 9th Division achieved great fame at Delville Wood through the feats of its South African brigade, whereas the 51st, after two failures against the German strong point at the south-east corner of High Wood, were taken out of the line in disgrace and sent to a quiet sector which was reserved for troops who were considered unfit for anything like real warfare. It was a sector afterwards held by the Portuguese army.

The 51st Division was commanded both in the attacks against the uncut wire at Festubert and in the failures at High Wood by an English engineer, Major-General G. M. Harper, who had gone out to France with the original Expeditionary Force as a Lieutenant-Colonel. After the failure at High Wood the whole of the B.E.F. knew the Division by the H.D. which was painted on guns, limbers, wagons, and steel helmets, and was universally interpreted as the initials of "Harper's Duds."

But although during 1915 and most of 1916 the two Scottish Divisions of Kitchener's army were far ahead of their territorial colleague in public fame and professional reputation, nevertheless the 51st possessed all the time an advantage which overwhelmed the other two, when at last it emerged into the limelight. For it was the only Division in the whole British army of which all the infantry wore kilts, and it was the only one to which the name Highland was attached. When, therefore, the 51st Division at last brought off a notable coup and stormed in November, 1916, the Y-ravine and the village of Beaumont-Hamel, the special correspondents sprang to arms with a whoop. At last they had something new to write about and they made the most of their opportunity. The romance of Inverlochy and Killiecrankie and Prince Charles Edward was reborn in the 51st Division, and on that day, November 13th, 1916, the 9th and 15th Divisions sank back into comparative obscurity and the Highland Division was lifted up to a pinnacle from which it was never allowed to descend until the war was over. It became the crack, storm-troop Division. The best of the kilted reinforcements were sent to it at the expense of the other two; the best of the remounts were to be found in its artillery horse-lines; whenever it attacked, it was supported by an immense force of heavy artillery; and remarkable legends were circulated not only throughout the rest of the B.E.F., but especially throughout the ranks of the 51st itself, of the toughness and the invincibility of the Division, and, above all, of the fear which its very name struck into the hearts of the adversary. Thus it was said, and universally believed, that a German instruction had been captured in which the British divisions were placed in a list in order of menace — much as lawn-tennis players are today often ranked in order of skill — and that on this list the Guards' Division was runner-up, to the Highland champions. "Harper's Duds" was hastily altered throughout the Army to "Harper's Devils," and a tradition of deep affection between these wild and magnificent mountaineers and their dapper English commander was quickly fostered. He was soon called, affectionately, "Uncle" by thousands of men who had not seen him a dozen times. The successive exploits of the Division at Arras, Ypres, and Cambrai, together with, and partly as a result of, the intensive propaganda, convinced the Highland infantry that they were invincible and that their commander was a great leader. So it was perhaps just as well that the survivors of those epic battles did not learn till many years after the war that "Uncle" Harper made two notable contributions to the tactics by which his division helped him to earn his fame.

Do not think for a moment that I am throwing stones at General Harper simply for the pleasure, keen though it is, which can always be derived from throwing stones at generals. General Harper is dead and was, I am sure, a gallant and charming man. But it is an essential point of this discussion to record his two tactical dogmas. Nor should it be thought that I am quoting from hearsay, rumour, or malicious slander. Both are matters of history.

In the first place, this engineer-colonel, on being appointed to the command of a division of infantry (with, of course, the field-guns and other attachments of a division), threw himself with gusto into the great machine-gun controversy, and threw himself in on the Kitchener side. That is to say, he sided with those who considered "three machine-guns per battalion ample, four a luxury." (In passing, surely this use of the word "luxury," in Kitchener's own writing, is one of the most remarkable pieces of irony on record.)

Towards the end of the war, Mr Lloyd George, a civilian who knew nothing about military affairs, succeeded in getting the number of machine-guns on a battalion front raised to sixty-four. But General Harper could not believe that a machine-gun was of any real use except in the hands of Germans. (Not even a general of the regular army could fail to notice, sooner or later, that a machine-gun in the hands of Germans was a very useful weapon indeed.)

The General's second dogmatic opinion was that tanks were no good. When, therefore, his division was taken out of the line in Flanders and sent to train with tanks for the surprise attack on Cambrai in November, 1917, "Uncle" was very lukewarm about the whole business. The resulting co-operation between tanks and Highlanders was sketchy, and to this sketchiness was due the disastrous check in front of Flesquières and the disorganisation of Haig's whole scheme of attack. Nor is it really a convincing defence of General Harper to say that Haig's whole scheme of attack was so utterly absurd that the disastrous check in front of Flesquières was a blessing in disguise, in that it saved the entire attacking force of six or seven divisions from being cut off and captured to the last man.

The fact remains that General Harper strongly disapproved of the only real defensive weapon of the war, and profoundly disbelieved in the only real offensive weapon. Yet the Highland Division were somehow persuaded to hold an implicit faith in the military ability of their English commander. It is almost as if the Highlanders had been led at Killiecrankie by Johnny Cope and had swept triumphantly into the fray because they had unbounded confidence in their leader. There is another point: the Highlander's traditional method of warfare was to attack at a great pace in mass. The clan was a corporate body and it attacked as a corporate body, shoulder to shoulder. Everything was staked on one throw. As I have already said, defensive fighting and rearguard action were outside the Highlander's technical and mental equipment. He had to win or lose quickly.

But the 51st Division gained its reputation in the World War by fighting of a very different sort. It was essentially a division of individuals, and it was never so dangerous, and it never achieved such startling results, as when its battalions lost all text-book formation and split up into handfuls of men. When operating in orthodox style, it was no better and no worse than any other. It was when it disintegrated into parties of twos and threes, or even better still, ones, that its great feats were performed. They did not require officers to command them on these occasions, nor the encouragement of the knowledge that they were part of a drilled and efficient organisation, with supporters on each side of them. All they had, and it was all they needed, was a sufficient sense of direction to keep their faces always turned towards the east where the Germans were, a fine idea of how to take cover from view and from bullets, and a resolution to keep on moving forward.

There is another curious phenomenon about this Division. It was very stubborn in defence. In the bad days of 1918, over and over again the 51st fought long and obstinate rearguard actions, almost invariably in the same small handfuls of independent individuals.

How can all those contradictions be reconciled? How can the history of the 51st Division be so written that it falls into place as a part of the history of the Highlands themselves? Is it possible to find a rational explanation of the extraordinary change which seems to have come over the character of the Gael? From being for centuries a mass-fighter, he suddenly becomes an individual fighter, and that, too, in a war which was essentially a mass-war; he suddenly develops an unheard of talent for stubborn defence; he drops his ancestral recklessness and becomes a cunning master of ruse and device; he fights as un-dramatically as possible; he only makes a move if it is likely to be a tactical success; he is practical and hard-headed; and, the most extraordinary changes of all, he has become a man who can be bamboozled into thinking that his English commander is a fine soldier; he has become a man who has travelled so far from regarding his Chief as his Father that he can regard an Englishman as his Uncle; a man who has inherited a superb ancestral valour and displays it in defeat after defeat that will go down in history as monumental examples of muddle and stupidity, but who, nevertheless, has inherited so little of the ancestral military instinct that he is easily persuaded that all the defeats have been victories.

It seems an insoluble problem to explain the change. But it is not. The answer is simple.

The Highland Division was largely composed of Lowlanders.

Out of the nineteen infantry battalions which at one time or another formed the brigades of the division, no fewer than twelve were recruited from areas on the Lowland side of the Highland Line.

The three brigades of artillery and most of the engineers were recruited in Aberdeen, Edinburgh, and Dundee, and comparatively few Gaelic clan-names appear in their rolls.

In fact, the Highland Division was really a Lowland Division with some Highlanders in it. And as the war went on and the original ranks grew thinner, the reinforcements contained only a small trickle from the north-west. And when the mere statistics are considered, it will be seen that this must be so. The glens, successively depopulated by Germans, English, and Chiefs, could not possibly have furnished enough men to maintain a division of 18,000 men on the Western Front at full strength throughout a series of assaults upon uncut barbed-wire and stoutly-fought machine-guns, and at the same time supply reinforcements to the Highland battalions in the 9th and 15th Divisions, and to the regular battalions of the Highland regiments, and at the same time provide a strong nucleus for the minesweepers. It was numerically impossible. And I fancy that it will ultimately be agreed that the chief Gaelic contribution to the man-power of the British efforts during the war was the work of the island fishermen among the mine-fields, rather than the valour of the handful of the infantry of the mountains. The fishermen were the remnant of the old blood, and, usually of the old Faith, crossing themselves in the reverse way because their Saint was crucified upside down; but the mountain-men, their brothers, had been scattered to the four winds, and their remnant was submerged by the levies of the industrial cities of the plains.

Once this fact is grasped, that the 51st Division was largely composed of Cymric Celts with only a sprinkling of Gaelic Celts, the whole story of the Division's outlook on life and behaviour in war falls neatly into place. Everything which was inexplicable and irrational when measured by the Gaelic scale, becomes clear and logical by the Cymric.

Thus the infantry did not attack like clans because they never had been clans. They fought like the stout Borderers of the days of Otterbourne, each for himself and no one afraid. Their defence in the March retreat of 1918, or at Soissons, or on the Lys, was the obstinate defence of Flodden. They fought to the last man, a thing no true Highlander would ever dream of doing. Their acceptance of an English general was an echo of the eleventh-century acceptance of the Anglo-Saxon and Norman Knights who crossed the hills to escape from the conqueror. Their refusal to understand that they had been defeated over and over again by the German machine-gunners was partly due to the Lowland refusal to admit defeat at the hands of anyone, and partly to their traditional ignorance of everything connected with the science of warfare except the actual individual use of arms. The history of the Anglo-Scottish wars of the fourteenth, fifteenth, and sixteenth centuries is one long tale of the military incompetence of the Scottish commanders and of the unflinching gallantry of the rank and file who were thus uselessly sacrificed. The Cymric Celt has never had the smallest objection to being slaughtered unnecessarily and has never borne any ill-will towards those who led him to the slaughter. The Gaelic Celt has always had the gravest objection to the former, and has always borne the keenest grudge against the latter. And it is interesting to notice, in passing, that the British soldier under whose command more lives were unnecessarily thrown away than under any other in our history was a Cymric Celt. Haig was in the true line of tradition from James IV as a strategist, and as a tactician, from Archibald Douglas the Regent, and from the later Regent, the Earl of Arran. What the Anglo-Saxon long-bow was to the earlier captains, the Germanic machine-gun was to the later. It may even be that the motto of the Haig family:

Betide, betide, whate'er betide,
Haig shall be Haig of Bemersyde,

is simply a polite and poetical way of saying that nothing can alter the essential characteristics of a typical Lowland family that has been born to command even though its members are without any of the talents requisite for success as a commander.

The Highland Division had other qualities which never saw their first light on the Gaelic side of the Line. Its infantry combined a dogged stolidity of temper with a capacity to laugh at adversity. They were not unduly depressed by mud or frost or dirt or insects. They had an almost Cockney power of producing a dry joke in unlikely circumstances. They saw no fundamental disgrace in having to do much digging and carrying. To the Highlander all navvying, whether in peace or in war, is undignified and unworthy of the profession of arms. And, lastly, the mounted units of the division took an especial pride in the welfare of their horses. The divisional artillery was famous for its gun-teams and wagon-teams. Now the Gael was never a horseman. He was, and had been for centuries, a foot-soldier. Even at Bannockburn the cavalry were under the command of the Lowland Keith, and the title of Earl Marshal, which is not a Celtic word but a Germanic word meaning "Servant of the battle-horses," came to Scotland by way of France from the Carolingian Kings, and was hereditarily vested in the Keiths. The influence of the Norman adventurers, and the more open nature of the south country, and the necessities of the English wars, combined to create a certain number of horse-soldiers among the Cymric Celts, and it was the descendants of the moss-troopers of the Border and of the Anglo-Saxons of the Lothians who cared for the horses of the 51st Division.

What was the effect upon the Gaelic remnant? What did the real Highlanders think when they first met their new brothers-in-arms, this tide of dour, stockily-built, stubborn soldiers, born fighters all, who marched to the new Raising of the Standard from Motherwell, Airdrie and Coatbridge, from Edinburgh, Dundee and Aberdeen, all wearing the kilt as to the manner born?

On the whole, I fancy that they felt nothing. The English and American tourists, the antics of Royalty at Balmoral, and the world-wide fame of Harry Lauder (it was the days before his knighthood) had accustomed them to anything. There were no more surprises. Everything that could be done to trample upon a race that once had been held in some esteem had already been done. Resistance, anger, aloofness, contempt, all had long ago been proved to be useless against the irresistible advance of a civilisation that was alien in spirit and only cousinly in blood, from the far distant past, and that had drawn for a thousand years so much of its inspiration from an Anglo-Saxon civilisation that was alien in both.

So the Highlander accepted without a murmur even the ultimate irony when the commands of the infantry battalions of the Highland Division were steadily filled with junior English cavalrymen, who had been finding promotion slow in the cavalry which was almost a noncombatant arm on the Western Front.

But the new wearers of the tartan saw nothing odd in the arrival of these Anglo-Saxon horsemen and their immediate promotion to commands. For they themselves were of the Cymry, and had understood the value of horses, although they would not, perhaps, have put horsemen to lead against bows and arrows as these Anglo-Saxon horsemen were put to lead against machine-guns. Furthermore, they were accustomed by tradition to accept the leadership of wandering adventurers who came from English armies, provided that they were of influential family and possessed their own horses.

But there was also a credit side. The exploits of the 51st Division brought a great deal of fame to the Highlander which he accepted with the same quietness and courtesy as he accepted all these strangers. He made no effort to disavow the vicarious glory which his cousins and their English friends so generously brought him. Indeed he basked in it, and enjoyed intensely the compliments which he had only partly earned. And so a curious, unofficial, indeed almost subconscious, bargain was struck. It was one of those bargains in which no words are spoken and no tangible cash passes from one hand to another, but in which both parties understand perfectly what is being arranged and both parties are perfectly satisfied. The Lowlander was to be allowed to wear the coveted panoply, to stand in the ranks of regiments that bore historic names, to be called a Highlander, and no questions asked. In return, he was to do nine-tenths of the fighting, and nine-tenths of the dying, and all the credit was to go to the Highlander, and no stones thrown. Each side made a contribution, the one putting their lives into the common pool, and the other putting glamour. Each side took something out of the common pool, the one an undeserved name, the other an unearned fame.

* * *

This strange passion of the Lowlander to be associated with a race which has had, for the last two hundred years, a steady record of failure and suffering, is due to a repressed desire which itself has been created by the growth of industrialism in the cities and small towns of the industrial areas. I shall explain in the next section of this book how that has come about. In so far as it affects the Lowlander's character it does not concern us here. But it has had consequences of deadly importance for the Highlander, for it has romanticised him. And that is a very different thing from making him romantic. Romance comes from within. Romanticisation is forced from without, and usually for the purpose of making money. It is the prelude to what is nowadays called a Sales-campaign. And the lay-figure upon which this process is forced ends by becoming a figure of tragedy, or a figure of fun. I do not say that the first Lowland desire to be allowed to mix with his poor relations had a commercial basis. Indeed I am going to prove a little later on that it had a purely sentimental basis. But the commercial side of it was not long in following, and it is that side which has been so disastrous. Sometimes it makes the Highlander a figure of fun, sometimes a tragic figure.

Take a couple of examples of how he and two of his most beautiful arts have been degraded until they have become a by-word and a laughing-stock: his music and his dancing.

The strange passion to be able to claim relationship with this unfortunate race is not confined to the southern parts of Scotland. During comparatively recent times it has reached certain quarters of London, and it is becoming common to hear, in a London drawing-room, ladies and gentlemen laying claim to a maternal grandmother from Kinlochmoidart, or to a great-grandmother who was a Chisholm of Glen Urquhart ("and so, of course, I'm entitled to wear the Chisholm tartan, my dear"), to connections, in fact, of varying remoteness with this clan or that. This is, in itself, an inoffensive foible. It does no one any harm, so far as I can see, and it must do a certain amount of good to tartan manufacturers and clan societies.

But rumours of this amiable and rather complimentary fad of the Sassenach have obviously reached certain individuals in the north who have a keen eye for profit and an elementary knowledge of the first eight bars of a very simple tune on the bagpipes. You may encounter them, if your luck is out, in the residential quarters of west or south-west London, or in the richer shopping streets. They haunt Mayfair, Belgravia, Westminster, Victoria, Kensington, and Earl's Court, always in couples and always using the same technique. They begin with a great clatter of noise to attract attention. Then they slip into their eight bars and play them execrably and hastily. As soon as that dubious part of the entertainment has been surmounted, they wind up with another great clatter and then hold out dingy glengarry-bonnets for sixpences. They wear kilts, of course, dingy and grimy, with moth-eaten sporrans and dirty spats, and the double effect of the dress and the ancient instrument is very lucrative. For it not only attracts the sixpences of the maternal granddaughters from Kinlochmoidart and the great-granddaughters of the Chisholm, but it has a hypnotic influence over another large section of the London community.

The cheapness of the modern motor-car, the excellence of the modern motoring-road, the increasing unpleasantness of life in Germany and the uncertainty of life in Austria, the truculence of Signor Mussolini, the fall of the pound, and the civil war in Spain, have all combined to divert a larger and larger number of English tourists to the north-west of Scotland during the summer and early autumn months. High pressure advertising and cheap excursion-fares on the railways have also played their part. In consequence London is crowded, during the late autumn, winter, and spring months with a citizenry which has, to use its own invariable phrase, literally steeped itself in the beauties of burn and loch and mountain-side and has passed a lot of its rainy afternoons in small hotels literally devouring, to use another of its phrases, the appropriate work of Mr H. V. Morton. To these, the sound of the bagpipes in the Brompton Road is like the hum of the heather-bee on Schiehallion or the merry cries of the golfers at Gleneagles. It is a reminder of the sound of motor-horns near the Forest of Achnacarry, or the click of cameras in the Pass of Brander. It brings back the memory of happy champagne-picnics by the Well of the Seven Heads on Loch Lochy, and the sound of the ill-played, furtive notes, coming in a south-westerly direction past Tattersall's, and Harrods, and Beauchamp Place, that latter-day Cranford, is greeted at a thousand Sunday luncheon-tables with the words: "Doesn't it remind you, my dear, of that day in Glengarry? You remember. The funny little valley where we lost the tin-opener and had to go on to that other place to buy a new one."

There is a tradition of humour in the south which makes piping a thing of fun. These seedy beggars, with their travesty of the music of the Gael, their bogus blowings and puffings, and their whining appeals for pennies after a moment or two of charlatanerie, make the Highlander understand how such a tradition of humour might possibly have arisen. These men bring disrepute and discredit upon the tartan and the music.

But the self-appointed descendants of the M'Crimmons are not the only ones who carry on the Gaelic torch. There are others.

Games can be very dignified and very noble. But in order to retain dignity and nobility they must take place in the country of their birth. So long as they are instinctive celebrations of the people of the soil, rejoicing for a moment on the ground where they work for the rest of the year and from which they gain their food, and their drink, their shelter, and their clothing, they are a kind of thanksgiving festival. But the moment they are transplanted to an alien soil which has no connection with their origin and no interest in the labour of those who take part, they lose all significance. They become simply a commercial enterprise, whether the commerce be the scrambling for shillings at the turnstiles by the promoters or the scrambling for money prizes among the competitors themselves. The Games of Ancient Greece, the Olympiads,

Nemeads, and the Pythiads which Pindar celebrated were far removed from the needlework contests and the crochet competitions of the Berlin Olympiad in 1936 with its grim background of political sadism and propaganda and persecution. The Highlands of Scotland also have their Games, although probably they were a relaxation of the warrior rather than the fertility worship of the agriculturist. Nevertheless they sprang from the people.

The new age has changed all that. It is true that it has not transplanted the games from their native soil. The new age is much too clever to make such a mistake. The preservation of the Highland Games in the old setting of glens and mountains and lochs is made part of the publicity arrangements of the new age whereby it hopes to lure ever-increasing numbers of tourists to patronise the hotels and the golf-courses of the north. The games on the new model are simply an adjunct of the railway posters, the hotel prospectuses, and the paragraphs in the Press about "the lure of the mountains," and the pictures of the shooting-parties on the moors. But the only part of the Highland Games which the new age has not changed is the soil. All else is as different from the festivals of the clans as Berlin is from Olympia. In the trials of strength and in the running, in the dancing, and the jumping, the competitors are in the main a band of professional athletes from all over Scotland, but especially from the neighbourhood of Glasgow, who travel from meeting to meeting. They are as much at home in the country of the Campbells as in the country of the Camerons, and perhaps even more at home still at the games in Braemar and Aboyne which are on their own Lowland side of the Line.

Whether or not they have an arrangement among themselves by which expenses and prize-moneys are pooled and results organised beforehand, I do not know. I certainly would not blame them if they had. After all, for them it is just as much a business as it is for the proprietors of the grouse-moors who wish to get a good tenant, and who wish, when they have got him, to please him with a little picturesque local colour. For without a doubt the games are picturesque. Marquees are pitched upon the green, and flags wave in the breeze, and there is a wide open space in the middle for the actual contests. The gentry from miles round promenade slowly about, many of them wearing kilts and plaids and carrying tall curly sticks, coming together for a momentary salutation, like those lovely little sea-horses in the tank in the aquarium in Regent's Park, and then drifting apart again in search of other friends. The rows of big cars, with number-plates of half the counties of England, glisten impressively, and the chauffeurs mingle derisively with the crowd. Side-shows offer the usual entertainments, and on the open space in the centre the brawny professionals, all in kilts, from whatever family they may derive their name or from whatever district they may hail, fling hammers and run races. On platforms, revolting little girls, in complete Highland dress and gay with curls and extra ribbons here and there, endlessly and self-consciously perform the lovely old dances.

It is perfectly true that the men who also dance the lovely old dances, dance them with grace and elegance. But my point is that they are roving professionals, making the tour of Oban, Inverness, Aboyne, Braemar, and the rest, just like the strong men and the runners. I do not blame them. They are there to make money. But I do blame those who have organised the games into part of the commercialisation of the glens.

The visitor from the south soon tires of the dancing, and even tires of pointing out how very sweet the little girls are. For the visitor there are two competitions which easily outbalance all the rest put together. It is these of which they will talk when they return to Manchester and Ealing, when the memory of sunsets over Moidart has faded from their minds and when the trail of the wounded deer has been forgotten and when even the delicious thud of the falling grouse on the heather is not so crisp and clear in the imagination as it once was.

These two competitions are, of course, Tossing the Caber, and the Best-dressed Highlander. The muscle-bound strong men heave and heave at the unpainted telegraph-pole which is, or appears to be, the substitute for the old fir tree, to the "oohs," and "aahs," and — I fear — often "ows" of the excited throng. And on the platform where the beastly little girls had disguised themselves as the soldiers of Killiecrankie, tailors' dummies continue the lamentable farce.

For the Highlander, and there will be many present, the only redeeming feature is the pipe-music. That alone is unchanging. That alone, while such men as Pipe-Major Ross, or John Macdonald of Inverness, are still alive and still piping, cannot lose its poetry, its gaiety, its dignity. And so by a grim irony, the only part of the Highland masquerade which the Southerner does not care for, does not understand, and, as a rule, does not even attempt to be civil about in ordinary conversation, is the only part which means anything at all. Sandow, or Zbysco, or the Terrible Turk would have won the strength competitions; Savile Row could dress the tailors' dummies, and any skilled team of tap-dancers from Alabama or the Carolinas could be trained to score heavily in the Reel of Tulloch. But only the blood of the mountains and the isles can maintain the line of the M'Crimmons.

*　*　*

But the pipers in the London streets and the Highland Games are only symptoms. They are not the disease itself. The disease is the Southern

Commercialisation of the glens. The charlatan pipers and the professional caber-tossers represent simply an aspect of the exploitation of the glens for the benefit of the south. They are in precisely the same category as the kilted regiments of the eighteenth century, Sir Harry Lauder's song "The Tangle of the Isles," and the massed pipe-bands at the Aldershot tattoo. They are bogus Romance, but they are big business.

All that is left of a race of soldiers is a handful of puppets and a slightly larger handful of flunkies. The puppets swagger along bravely in their finery and are carefully applauded by the people who have lured them into puppetry. The flunkies have usually even discarded their finery, and too often dress their flunkeydom in the dull dress of their southern masters.

For that is what the Highlands have become. A place of Highland flunkeys and Anglo-Saxon lords. It is a sports ground in which the poor, to whom the land was once communal under the Chief, can get no sport but only some toil for the alien. Go into the smoking room of any London club in July and you will hear the conversation — if conversation it can be called — soon veer round to the moors. The prospects, the rain in the spring, the state of the heather, the rents, the quaint sayings of the old keepers, the queer accounts of the gillies, the charm of whisky on a hill-side (with the inevitable, and wrong, statement from some wiseacre that "it is the peat-water which makes the whisky"), reminiscences of immense bags capped by reminiscences of other immense bags, the bad shooting of old So-and-so and the brilliant shooting of old what's-his-name, and the note of genuine sadness that so many lovely spots should be desecrated by Americans and Jews, and sometimes a combination of the two, all this and more you will hear from the business-men, and the military men, and the rich, idle young men, in the West End clubs in July. The Englishman sincerely laments this invasion of Americans and Jews. He fears not only that the immemorial privilege of his race to possess all available sporting facilities is being infringed, but also in a queer, roundabout way he feels that the "Scotch" are not getting a square deal. He feels the "Scotch" are delighted to see him each year at the beginning of August, because all the world loves not only a lover, but an English sportsman perhaps even more than a lover; but it is a bit unfair that they should be saddled with such fearful outsiders. The English sportsman does not often pause to think that it was he himself who set the fashion of tree-planting and deer-killing, or that it does not really matter to the man who has lost everything, land, clan, chief, independence, and all, whether the sporting intruder is a descendant of Boss Croker, Judas Iscariot, or Edward the First. They are all intruders by right of money into a land which none of them could conquer by might of the sword save only the German Cumberland. The English may swear at the American who scatters champagne-bottles all over the moors to the left of him, and at the Jew who wears bright yellow boots and misses every bird on the moors to the right of him. But all are fundamentally the same. To the Highlander who has been driven, or has fled, from the glens, he is the barbarian whose presence is a monstrosity; to the Highlander who has remained behind, he is a source of income for a few weeks which must be made to last the entire year, a god-sent creature to whose innumerable guests the palm must be out-stretched obsequiously and humbly, a hero whose financial status puts him on a moral level with the Lords of the Isles and the Captain of Clanranald. The land has been bought, and the survivors of the men have sold themselves to go with it.

But even here a little dignity has been saved. It is true that the men have sold themselves, but they have gone with the land. They still tread the hill-sides with all the outward appearance of free men. They are still concerned with the same activities as their forefathers, the manly business of hunting and fishing, of carrying a gun and following a stag. They may not often fire the gun or land the fish, but at least they look as if they still owned the world. No one has yet succeeded in driving them in large numbers into new factories, or in turning them into willing navvies.

Not even the lavish expenditure of Mr Lever, the late Lord Leverhulme, could corral them into his soap-works in the Island of Harris. Yet that enterprising and go-ahead industrialist from Oldham, in Lancashire, spared no pains and omitted no detail which might tempt the Gael into co-operation with the new Port Sunlight. He took the hamlet of Obbe, in Harris, and rechristened it Leverburgh, a name pleasingly reminiscent of the patron's own name and of the great Scottish names of Edinburgh, Jedburgh, Dryburgh, and Roxburgh; he spent thousands of pounds and was prepared to spend thousands more; he even went so far in his desire to charm the stubborn hearts of the islands and the ocean seaboard as to accept from the Government in Whitehall, in return for his services to commerce, party, and empire, the title of Baron Leverhulme of the Western Isles. But all was in vain. The men who had meekly accepted the recruiting-sergeant, the sheep, the deer, and the sportsman, jibbed suddenly at the soap-king.

Once before, as we have seen, a very large sum of money had been refused for a betrayal — thirty pieces of paper, in fact, if thousand-pound notes were in existence in 1746 — and Mr Lever suffered the same indignity as George the Second in seeing his munificence rebuffed with scorn.

What was the reason for this sudden jibbing at a large sum of money? It could not have been that the Gael dislikes material possessions. He does not. He was always ready to desert Charles Edward in order to stow away in the safe place a couple of stolen cows or the loot from a battlefield, just as he is always ready to accept a ten-shilling note for his services to a sportsman. He may not be as able as his Cymric cousin in acquiring wealth through the exploitation of industry and finance, or as able as his Irish brother in acquiring wealth through the control of municipal politics in America, but on a smaller scale he is as ready as they to possess a share of whatever swag is going, provided that he does not have to do manual labour to get it.

There must have been some reason for his refusal to share in the prosperity which Mr Lever would have brought to Obbe from Oldham. It is agreed that it was loyalty to Charles Edward which impelled the first great refusal to be bribed. Was it loyalty to something else which impelled the second? I should like to think, for example, that it was loyalty to the loveliness of the Highlands and Islands, and a passionate desire to keep the chimneys, as well as the spirit, of Oldham out of the Hebrides. But there is no evidence for this. Still more should I like to think that it was loyalty to the ancient title of Lord of the Isles which the soap-baron was so near to getting, that to all intents and purposes he did get it. There is no doubt that a wave of indignation, or as close to indignation as the servants and the tenants of the new kings of the deer-forests dare to be moved in these precarious days of month's notices and unemployment, swept across the north when it was announced that a Welsh Prime Minister had handed, in London, the barony of the Western Isles to a man from Lancashire. There was a small change in the wording, but the essence of the title was the same. The Lordship of the Isles! That immeasurably ancient name! That name so great! That name which carried with it a splendour so bright and so burnished, like the Atlantic itself as it rolls gently up to the Isles on a summer evening when the sun is going down! That name so deep in its significance to the whole life and history of those early Gaelic Celts who looked to the islands for their ancestors and for their faith which had come to them from across the sea!

So profound was the meaning of the great title and so violent and passionate were the rival claims to it, that as early as the beginning of the sixteenth century it had fallen into abeyance, partly because the claimants were too evenly matched to reach a final conclusion and partly because the kings feared its power and were resolute in preventing its revival.

But although it had been a ghost for centuries, perhaps because it had been a ghost for centuries, it had become a legend as well. It had become a symbol of the Golden Age of the west, when the Gael ruled over Gaeldom, and when there was one faith, the faith which had come to Iona from Ireland, in all the land of Albainn from Ben Lomond to Loch Torridon and from Barra to the Monadliath Mountains. The Lordship of the Isles had died before the bad times came to the west, and so it was never tainted with all the things which filtered across the hills from Edinburgh by way of Inveraray and Geneva.

And then suddenly it was resuscitated, with a trivial alteration, in a political office near Whitehall, and was clapped with a coronet on to the head of a rich soap-maker of Lancashire.

I would like to believe that this is the true reason for the revolt, that it was the Honour of the Isles which was being defended. It would mean not merely that the ancient spirit had not entirely died out, but that the ancient spirit had really existed. It would mean that the remnant which had survived in its ancestors the guns and ropes of the butcher, and in its own generations the sheep and the deer of the Chiefs and the English, still preserved in its misty subconsciousness a memory of Donald of the Isles and Somerled. It would mean that, perhaps after all, the Gaelic race in Scotland is indestructible.

But before we accept this solution, so gratifying to the pride of any Highlander, we must in all fairness consider another possibility.

Mr George Blake has written:

"We may wonder at the precise nature of the forces that obliged a very able and active and generous man to retire from the fray. Was it mere local resentment of the Sassunach intrusion? Was it laziness, as some cruelly say? Or was it — and this is a question of immense interest and importance — the clash of a romantic and aristocratic with a realistic and acquisitive tradition?

"All the elements suggested were probably behind that sensational defeat of industrialism: one of the most significant episodes in Scottish history. But we have to give the Highlander credit for a distinguished philosophy at the back of his behaviour in this strange business. It was no doubt unconscious, but it told him that the making of money is not all, and that it profits a man nothing if he gain the whole world and lose his own soul at the same time."

I cannot believe that the cause was "local resentment of the Sassunach intrusion." The Sassunachs had been intruding on the mainland for at least two generations and local resentment had not flared up. Nor do I think that a romantic tradition clashed with an acquisitive tradition. It certainly did not, as we have seen, when men like Mackenzie of Kintail sold their land to men like Winans. But I do think that Mr Blake might be nearer the solution if he separated the two words, "romantic and aristocratic."

From time immemorial the feathered, kilted, male of the clans was a warrior and not a drudge. He disliked manual labour intensely and always preferred that the heavy toil should be done whenever possible by his women, and it may have been this instinctive habit, descending from father to son from the beginning of history down to the fatal year of 1746, which defeated Mr Lever of Port Sunlight. Perhaps it was not the ghost of Somerled which inspired the resistance, but the spectre of a day's work in a factory. Since 1746 the men of the Highlands and Islands have toiled endlessly on their land and at the fisheries, but not for the sake of gain. Sheer hunger drove them to it. They have worked because they had to. Lord Leverhulme offered them a means of making more than a bare livelihood, of working to earn pocket-money in addition to bread, of raising themselves from the back-breaking serfdom of the agriculturist to the high estate of the factory hand. Perhaps this was more than they could stand. For it implied that a Highlander would work without the compulsion of hunger, and might even — who knows — sink to the level of enjoying work and taking a pride in it. That would bring in the "aristocratic" tradition. To work to live is natural; to work for more money than is necessary to live is not the act of a gentleman. With that sense I might find myself in agreement. But whether it was pride in the ancient glories of the Isles that inspired the resistance or whether it was an instinctive dislike of hard work, the fact remains that no Port Sunlight or Leverburgh arose in the island of Harris, and so we cannot, fortunately, paraphrase G. K. Chesterton and write "from evening isles fantastical rings far the evening siren."

I wish I could think it was Somerled. But I am afraid I think it was laziness.

CHAPTER V

Industry and the Glens

I will briefly relate one more episode in the story, and then we can turn at last to the character of the men who have lived and made this story.

I have chosen for this last episode a debate in the House of Commons in March, 1937, partly because it brings this historical sketch up to date, and partly because it is a perfect illustration of the way in which different forces, conflicting interests, and outside pressures, continue to be exerted on the Highlands. The fate of the country lies today, as it has lain for centuries, in the hands of the aliens. They have the power, and they have most of the land, and there is no defence for the Highlanders against arbitrary and irrational decisions taken by men whom he has never heard of, sitting in the capital city of another country.

The debate about which I am writing was on a Private Bill to establish a calcium carbide factory on the chain of Highland lochs which run from Fort George to Fort Augustus. The proposal was to build a factory at the head of one of the lochs and to dig a tunnel from the main chain westwards to the Atlantic for the purpose of providing hydraulic power. The factory would be only a beginning of a huge scheme which would ultimately consist of many factories dotted over the neighbourhood.

The Company itself had a directorate almost exclusively composed of Englishmen. Its factories would certainly destroy the amenities of Scotland's noblest glen, and at the same time it would unquestionably create a large amount of employment in the distressed areas north of the Highland Line, and would bring in a large sum of money in wages and a greatly increased spending power throughout Inverness-shire.

The supporters and opponents were curiously ranged. On the one side was, of course, the English Company backed by about half of the Inverness-shire County Council, including Sir Donald Cameron of Lochiel, and by Mrs Flora Macleod of Macleod, and by Sir Alexander MacDonald of Sleat. Against the proposal was, firstly, the Inverness Town Council, headed by its Provost, Hugh

Mackenzie; secondly, that amorphous body of vague idealists up and down the country who prefer the beauty of a glen to the smell of calcium-carbide; and, thirdly, a sprinkling of gentlemen from South Wales who naturally could not help noticing that if the factory was not built in the Highlands on hydraulic power it would probably be built in South Wales on coal power.

In the Debate on the second reading there was one genuine Highlander who opposed the scheme, Sir Murdoch MacDonald, the member for Inverness. He was supported by a member of the famous Lowland family of Ramsay (an ancestor of his must surely have been the famous Ramsay of Dalwolsy, who helped the great Douglas to hold the Border against the English six hundred years before), and Sir Murdoch's other ally was a Socialist from Glasgow called Davidson (the Davidsons of Invernahaven in Badenoch were connected with the Clan Macintosh and are generally regarded as a sept of the Clan Chattan).

In favour of the Bill were the son and heir of the great Lowland family of Hamilton which is the senior branch of the family of Douglas, a Lowland gentleman from Aberdeen, a former Secretary of State for Scotland from Fife, a Socialist Lowlander from Stirling, an Englishman from Sheffield, and the present Secretary of State for Scotland, himself a citizen of Lanark.

More important from the historical and social points of view than any of these was the support given to the Bill by the member for the Western Isles, a Macmillan, and the member for Caithness, one of the Chieftains of the Norman clan of Sinclair.

It is the same old story. The destinies of the glens are in the hands of the aliens and the Chiefs. The English want to build their factories, and it is a Macleod of Dunvegan, a Cameron of Lochiel, and a Sinclair Chieftain who will encourage them, and the land for the sites will be land that is owned, or was once owned, by the Chiefs. A clause in the Bill provided for the compulsory expropriation of smallholders who were reluctant to leave their land, and so the wheel continues to run in exactly the same old groove. The clansmen left their lands to fight for their Chiefs. They were then driven out to make room for sheep, then to make room for deer. There is no change of heart or change of procedure. The only change is from sheep to deer, and from deer to calcium-carbide. And the crowning irony of the situation was that the British Parliament, with its overwhelming majority of English members, rejected the Bill by 188 votes to 140, and saved, for a time at any rate, the Great Glen from English chemicals.

CHAPTER VI

The Highlander's Instinct for Drama

So now at last we come to the point. What manner of man is it who has lived through these vicissitudes, who has fought and lost so many battles, who has made so much poetry and so much music, who has dreamed so many dreams and brought none of them to fulfilment except only one, and that the greatest of them all, the rebirth of the race in Canada? Is there a consistent thread running through the story? Is there a common ground beneath the triumphs and the failures? Is there, in fact, any one characteristic, or set of characteristics, which can be written down as essentially and fundamentally Gaelic, and which can be used as a scale by which to measure, or a tag by which to explain, the contradictions and confusions?

I think there is.

I think that every action, every thought, every emotion, of the Highlander is, and always has been, governed, guided, and inspired by a passionate love of Drama. His life must be a spectacle, not necessarily for an audience to look at but for himself to look at. Indeed the play is better without an audience, for your true actor is independent of applause. He lives in a world that is far removed from the world of every day, and no one is more astonished than he when he is told, as I am now telling him, that the curtain is down, and that the house is empty, and that the till is empty, and that the lovely company of his friends has been disbanded long ago, and that nothing is left for his race except the scenery, and the costumes, and the time that has to be passed before death comes.

The background of the Highlander's life is dramatic. He was born on a stage of magnificent scenes. In summer the mountain-sides are purple with the heather or golden with the whin and the broom or dotted with the red whortleberry, and in winter the snow lies heavily on the pinewoods. Half the year is soft and scented and gay, and half is hard and cruel. Both are dramatic. There are no half-tones. The colours are brighter on Iona than anywhere else, and the moonlight upon the Isles is full of Celtic mystery, and the great eagles drop slowly down the sides of the Coolins, and the glens are full of the sounds of little streams. It is all pure theatre.

Nature is heightened, made more vivid, more intense, by just that small iota which changes life into art. And, to match his background the Highlander has changed himself, or has been changed — for it is partly conscious and partly subconscious — into a being who must live vividly and therefore artificially. It is perfectly possible to be vivid and natural, which is a very different thing. All great men and women are always both. It is, in fact, the stamp of genius. But the man who must be vivid, and who puts all the emphasis on the word "must," is bound to be artificial, for he is forcing himself all the time on to his own private stage whether he has collected an audience or not. Once this fact is grasped, that the Highlander is an actor first, last, and all the time, everything about him becomes clear and consistent.

He has the mountains behind him and he calls them by wonderful romantic names like Cruachan, and the Shepherd of Etive, and Schiehallion; he calls the islands Benbecula or Colonsay or Oronsay, and he calls the little arms, by which the Atlantic laps round Skye, the Sound of Sleat and the Kyle of Loch Alsh. All these are his scene. He has designed his costume to match. There was never a male panoply to equal for sheer theatricality the full-dress kilt. And its "props" are on the same brilliant level of theatrical fantasy. Not even the most dashing Regency buck or Restoration fop ever thought of carrying more than one sword when he entered polite society. The Highlander is incompletely dressed, by his own standards, unless he carries three, one on his right hip, one at his left side, and one in his stocking. His ancestral lace must be secured with a diamond pin and his snuff mull must be horn and silver and cairngorm. But, as I have already pointed out and emphasised, it is a male costume, the costume of a fighting man who is not concerned with manual labour. It is three swords that he carries, not three spades, or three spanners. And that is significant. For the kilt, and the overwhelming sense of drama, and the passionate desire to be taken for a soldier and not mistaken for a farmer, are all simply manifestations, in an intense form, of the masculine character. They are nothing else but different ways of strutting. They are, in fact, simply the tail-spread of the peacock.

Here, with the peacock, we reach another important stage in the argument. The Highlander, with his gaudy dress, and his superb swagger, can strut upon his stage and amuse himself, but in his heart he knows that he is only rehearsing. He has this distinction over other actors — as is only natural, for the Highlander must have an outward and visible distinction over all other men; otherwise his reason for existence vanishes — that his rehearsal is always a dress-rehearsal. Again there are no half-tones. There is no acting in mufti. There may be no one else in the theatre, but he himself is there. But it is only a rehearsal. He is waiting to play to a house that shall be filled with women, even if only one woman is in it. One woman can fill a house, just as one woman can fill a world. That is the ultimate end of the Highlander's swaggering. That is the secret.

It must be so. A sense of drama, whether it be fostered by oceans and mountains, or by eagles and eagles' feathers, or by a wild love of colour, comes in the end to one thing and to one only, a sense of the beauty which might exist and which ought to exist. The drama is not life; it is life as it ought to be. It is a picture of the world as it would have been if Shakespeare had been God. There would be terrors and tragedies, but they would be compact with terrible beauty and tragic beauty. There would be hell in the world under Shakespeare's regime, just as there is hell in the world now under God's. But the bald-headed yokel from Stratford could never have made the sordid, dirty, squalor, or the endless, rewardless, toil, or the dull misery of unrequited love. His poor, his labourers, his lovers, were beautiful.

The Highlander's instinct for drama has made him search either for beauty everywhere or for despair, and he has found both in many places. But for men who are in love with these two there is only one ultimate standard of beauty and that is to be found in woman. Colour may be harsh, music discordant, snow muddy, friendship erratic. But there is always some sort of beauty in every woman, and that is a universal truth. So the Highlander's self-conscious masculinity has grown more and more intense, because he has known, somehow, that the whole basis of human life is an intense feminity. He and the peacock are blood-brothers. Both spend their lives in an unceasing attempt to be impressive, in order to impress their woman, and so both only succeed in being rather childish.

The Highlander's kilt is the child's love of dressing-up; his sense of drama is the child's love of pretending. His woman, of course, is not in the least impressed. No woman ever is impressed by that sort of thing. But she accepts his childishness and finds it rather endearing, as women always do. She allows him to wear the lovely dress and to play the lovely music and to dance the lovely dances. She even allows him to fight the useless battles, and does not object to his manly insistence that she should perform the heavy labour and not he. The Highlander holds the centre of the stage, because she does not want to be on his stage at all. Being a woman, and therefore universal, she has better things to do than to spend the whole day acting. And anyway she knows that he is only trying to please her in his childish way.

* * *

But his stage has not the naturalness of the child. It is artificial because it is self-conscious. Other nations, other men, all over the world, have had the natural, and rather childish, instinct to "conquer or die." The Highlander's instinct is artificially dramatic. It is to "conquer or be conquered." And better still is the logical development of that idea which is "conquer or do not resist at all." The first is shown at Bannockburn where he helped the victory in dramatic fashion — his infantry attack against archers, cavalry, and men-at-arms was unprecedented — and at Prestonpans where he won dramatically, and at Culloden where he ran away dramatically. He had to be sensational, whether going forwards or backwards.

The second idea is shown when he was confronted with lawyers and their documents. He saw no chance of conquering, so he did not resist. The Duke of Sutherland and other sheep-mad Chiefs who evicted the clansmen won a bloodless battle. The moment that the clansmen found themselves with their backs to the wall, they obeyed orders meekly and went away. They put up no fight. And it was the same when the English grouse-shooters and deer-stalkers invaded the glens. The clansmen touched their hats civilly and accepted the invaders and their wages and their tips. Their line of least resistance was the line of no resistance. When the Highlander was evicted from his poor cottage, he made no fuss. He went quietly. A legal document was to him as powerful a weapon as an Anglo-German cannon. He was devoted to his land, and he would almost face death for it, but he would not face a writ for it. There was always something about the grim, distant, shadow of the law, whether it was law made in Edinburgh, which was bad, or in London which was worse, or in Inveraray which was the worst of all, that daunted the Gael. He lost heart when he was confronted with it. Aberdeen advocates or Writers to the Signet could march triumphantly where Hessians and Hawleys had bolted. The quill was a great deal stronger than the dirk.

* * *

Here, I think, is the moment to compare the two blood-brothers of the Gaelic race, the Irish and the Scots. The common ground on which a comparison can be based is the word "eviction." For in that word is bound up the whole attitude of a peasant people to the land. Sentiment, livelihood, religion, law, patronage, fertility, all come from the land. And eviction cuts at the root of everything.

The peasant may worship his land. But the test comes when he is asked what he will do to save it from strangers. That is the time when his protestations of centuries of devotion will be measured by a practical scale. In other words, his bluff, if bluff it is, will be called.

Both the Scottish and the Irish Gael have been fighting a long battle for their land against the English. The Scottish method was to fight spectacular battles with their soldiers in long shining rows, once or twice in a century. The Irish method was passive resistance interspersed with assassination. The Scot was a master of useless attacks, the Irish of deadly ambushes. The former wore his own costume in bright colours when he fought, the latter wore a drab travesty of the English dress. The former's attempts to gain independence were spasmodic and quickly discouraged by a defeat; the latter's were unending and undefeatable.

And it is important to remember that the Irish not only fought for their freedom in the fields. They took the trouble to master the English technique of parliamentary government in the Englishman's own parliament, of which he is so proud, and to try to win their freedom by defeating him at his own game. By the time that Parnell was laying ambushes behind Standing Orders, and sniping from the shelter of Rules of Procedure, the Scots had given up the game and were either gillies or emigrants.

The Irish are essentially a tougher, harder-headed, more practical race. To murder a landlord or an agent whom you dislike was to them an obvious thing to do. In Scotland it was so rare that the murder of Campbell of Glenure was a major sensation.

Both races have been instinctively fascinated by drama, and there again the fundamental difference comes out. The Highlander has always loved the theatre, but he has loved it as an actor. The Irishman loves it as a writer. The one is busy enjoying himself in the ephemeral triumph of holding the centre of the stage. The other sees nothing worth while in that, and prefers to aim at the more practical advantages of literary immortality. Up to twenty or thirty years ago there was almost no theatre of Scottish literature, but there have been plenty of Scottish romances in real life. The real life of Ireland for the last few hundred years has been dismal and drab, but it has produced a long series of famous dramatists.

Again, take the use of words. Both the Irish and the Scots have an instinctive love of the sound of words. For centuries the Scot used his own language, whereas the Irish adopted the language of the conqueror. The result is that Gaelic literature is almost unknown outside the glens or Canada, whereas the Irish by their practical adoption of a world language have ensured a world circulation of their poems, their plays, and their ideas.

As in warfare, as in poetry, as in the struggle for independence, so it was also in emigration. When the new world was opened to the flood of emigration in the nineteenth century, the Scots sentimentally preferred to go to Canada where some of their fathers and grandfathers were already settled, whereas the Irish, hard-headed and unsentimental, went straight to the United States where the opportunities for getting rich were incomparably greater. The Irish were the first people in the nineteenth century to understand that for a vigorous and ambitious youth there was no place in the world to match the United States. Again, they were the first people to realise that the ordinary route to the top of the tree in the United States could easily be reversed and that Wealth could be achieved by Power much more easily than the other way about. Again, they were the first to realise that Power in the United States can more easily and profitably be attained through Municipal Politics rather than through Federal or State Politics. And the Irish, with their clear political vision, saw that the broad basis on which to build Municipal Power was the Police Force. The control of New York by means of the superb organisation of Tammany Hall, the control of Boston and Chicago and many another American city, is built upon the simple Irish cop. The gigantic fortunes of men like Boss Croker, Boss Tweed, Boss Murphy, consisted simply of loot stolen from the people by means of the Municipal Power resting upon the simple Irish cop, and when at last the classes in America which ought to have been called the ruling-classes turned over in their long sleep and thought they might do a little ruling themselves, they found the dreamy, unpractical, visionary Irishman firmly entrenched with scarp and counterscarp, bastions, lunettes, moats, in the heart of the main municipal fortresses.

There was also another consideration which influenced the direction of the two rivers of emigration. The Scots, in spite of the '45, and in spite of the devastations of Butcher Cumberland, and in spite of the coming of the English ideas to the north, did not feel sufficiently strongly about their own independence to want to escape from the British flag. So they had no real objections to remaining within the Empire. The Irish had been so bitter for centuries and had kept the bitterness alive with such determination that they found in the United States the ideal escape from the domination of the English. The Irish were never defeatist. Their record of indomitability is perfectly consistent, and if ever English politicians would grasp that simple little historical truth, the relation between Britain and Ireland would be very greatly simplified.

The common factor, and at the same time the dividing factor, in the history of the two branches of the Gaelic race, the Irish and the Scots, has been the impact of the English. They might have run side by side, and developed on parallel lines, had it not been for this impact. But whereas the English were resisted and stubbornly driven back, century after century, by the Lowland Scot while the Highlander lurked proudly but ineffectively in his glens, in Ireland the entire brunt fell upon the Gael. There was no Lowlander in Ireland until Ulster was planted with the scum of Calvinism, and then, of course, it was a pro-English scum. The Gael had to stand by himself against the

English. And, alone of all the nations of the earth, except for the Americans, black, white, red, yellow, or brown, Christian or atheist, "baptised or infidel," the Irish Gael has fought the Englishman to a standstill and defeated him. It has taken him seven hundred years, but he has done it. The mere fact that it has taken him seven hundred years, quite apart from his ultimate victory, is infinitely to his credit. No one else, except the French, has kept the battle alive half so long, and the French have almost always been defeated. The Irish and the Americans, alone in history since 1066, have been aggressively victorious in the end. The Lowland Scot was defensively victorious for many hundred years, but what he stubbornly denied to the armies of the Plantagenet he tamely handed to the politicians of Queen Anne, and so, as I shall show in a later part of this book, threw it all away. The Highlander went down quickly and was soon enrolled in the ranks of the conqueror, and was soon so lost to ancestral shame and tradition that he was fighting for the conqueror against France. In a later age many Highland soldiers exceeded even this ignominy and fought for the conqueror against the Irish. But here there was no opportunity for dashing charges, and the system of ambushes was victorious.

* * *

When, therefore, it comes to facing the world, the Irishman prefers old clothes and victory. The Highlander is less concerned with the choice between victory and defeat, so long as he may wear fine clothes. His stage is more important than his battlefield, and his stage-manager than his general. (There is only one dramatic accessory who is not essential to him, and that the prompter. The words will always come easy.)

It is not that the Highlander is driven to his theatrical display by an inferiority complex. As I have shown, there is another and much more powerful reason for it. There is hardly another race in the world, except the French — and the two have much in common — which is so acutely conscious, whether rightly or wrongly is another matter, of its own superiority. When Glengarry was invited by the Lord Mayor of London to move his seat at a banquet and come nearer to the top of the table and he replied that where Glengarry sits is the top of the table, he genuinely believed it. He was not trying to be funny. He was stating a truth that had been evident to him for a thousand years. I would like to think that it is this feeling of superiority which has helped to steer the Gael to disaster. I would like to think that it is the old feeling that gentlemen do not fight with cads, either with the cad's weapons or with their own, nor, if Fate loads the dice against him, does a gentleman play against loaded dice. Is his refusal to descend into the arena caused by his dislike of dust? I am afraid not. I am afraid it is simply the same old story, that the childish joy in the theatre has made him equally ready to be a conqueror or a defeatist, provided that he can be one or the other on the grand scale. He is equally ready to write an Ode of Triumph or a Lament. John Graham of Claverhouse was far more useful by riding a great black horse and getting killed with a silver bullet than by being victorious. If Prince Charles Edward had arrived in Moidart with an army of French professional soldiers he would have served his Jacobite supporters better than by arriving with six friends, but the Gael would have lost the immortal scene in Glenfinnan.

And if Charles Edward had been victorious, his infantrymen would have been much less happy, in the long run, in the streets of London than in the legend of Flora Macdonald and the thirty thousand pounds.

It is all symbolised in the gaiety of the dance-music of the pipes, which is the Highlander at his best when the sun is shining, and in the Lament, which is the Highlander at his most poetical in defeat. Gaiety or despair, there is no half-way house between them. But there must be colour and drama in both. Even when the children of heroes were dumbly allowing themselves to be flung out of their cottages, they succeed in raising their dumb acquiescence to a tragic dignity by the simple device of taking an old Lament for the pipes and giving it the wonderful name "Lochaber No More." Was there ever a more tragic epitaph in three words on a whole race? Was ever an act of defeatism so subtly elevated into nobility? And it was done with the minimum of trouble. The Lament was composed in 1694 and was originally called "King James Marches to Ireland." The hearts of the emigrants might be breaking, but not to the extent of going to the trouble of composing a new tune.

The whole character rings true at every turn. It is always consistent. It is always simple and transparent. There is nothing dramatic in manual labour, so manual labour is taboo; there is nothing dramatic in the admission that you have been defeated by a better man than yourself, so defeats must be avoided and, when regrettably incurred, must be glossed over by the invention of some dramatic detail; there is nothing dramatic in inactivity — the very word Drama is from the Greek word for Action — so the Highlander is always and for ever restless, seeking out some new thing to do, some, new sensation to make, some new spectacle to stage. He must have the limelight shining on him, either as the hero of some epic feat or of some unparalleled disaster. He must either lead the world, or be the victim of fate, and that is why he will never keep step. To keep step implies doing something in exactly the same way as your neighbours; it implies agreeing that your neighbours are in the right about something; it implies the submergence of individuality; it implies an acquiescence in a common policy. All these things are anathema to the Highlander because they are undramatic. They are like living in a villa in a row of villas. The Highlander must either live in a sensational palace, or he must stand with folded arms, haughtily watching his thatched cottage being burnt to the ground by an overwhelming force of aliens. He would become a Prime Minister, or he would go to the scaffold for murdering a Prime Minister. But he would never run the risk of a month's imprisonment for non-payment of rates. For people would giggle at the sight of the Eagle-fathers in Brixton jail, and the giggles of strangers are death to the clansmen.

It is possibly this deadly fear of justified ridicule that makes him so punctiliously honest about the small, everyday businesses of the day such as paying bills, repaying loans, telling lies, being courteous, and so on. He is in mortal fear of being made to look a fool when he knows in his heart that he has been a fool. Towards unjustified ridicule he has a magnificent indifference. So long as he is at peace with his own conscience, the outer world cannot harm him. He is supremely self-confident. But the moment he loses that self-confidence in the knowledge that he has done something ridiculous, then he stands in a great dread of giggles.

He very seldom really loses his temper in the sense in which your English colonel or general will "foam at the mouth" or "see red." Partly it may be that he does not think anything is worth the honour of having aroused him to anger. Or it may be that calmness in adversity is in itself a heroic quality and therefore one that should be carefully cultivated by actors. On the other hand he is very easily irritated by trifles. The reason for this is obvious. When a man is acting the leading part in an epic drama which is no less than the story of his life, there ought to be some guardian angel watching over him and keeping trifling worries away from him.

The picture of Alen Breck Stewart, in Stevenson's *Kidnapped*, seems to me to come nearer to the truth about the Gael than any other I know. Poetry and pettiness, swordsmanship and pride and irritability, generosity and vanity, and a sort of mental and spiritual and physical flamboyance, these are among his essential qualities. By flamboyance, I do not mean the boastful swagger of the Gascon. The Highlander is too conscious of his own real character to be boastful. It took the great fight in the Round House to drag the simple, modest question from Alan Breck's lips: "Oh man, am I no a bonny fighter?" But the Gael is flamboyant in the sense that he is alive. Stagnation is repellent to him because any form of stagnation is the antithesis of all drama. When things are stagnant no man can be either first or last, and he must always be one or the other.

He even has a very genuine reason for drinking so much alcohol as he undoubtedly does. The ordinary man drinks in order to escape from the dullness of his ordinary life, or from his cares, or from his bills, or from his wife, or from his absence of a wife. He drinks on the vague chance that he may see high visions and people his world with heroes, though, of course, he very seldom does. But the Gael, whether he be Scots or Irish, drinks in order to escape from the dust of the stars and a world of heroes. It is his only way of being dull and drab for an hour or two. Otherwise his dreams of the beauty which might come to him, of the beauty which is always just above his head, but which might come down a little or to which he might rise a little, would drive him mad. Or perhaps he is mad already.

Of minor qualities, he loves bright colours and music, and poetry; he is hospitable and, unless severely crossed, courteous; he is fond of dancing and laughing and drinking; he often has brains but finds it much easier to let his powers of acting do the work for him; he despises in his heart all those who are taken in by the glamour of his past, and of his clothes, and of his institutions. But, although he despises everyone who is deceived by the glamour, he never for a moment stops trying to deceive them. He has a wonderful line in what is now called Sales-Talk, and he has used it to try to make the world envious of his ancestry. He has something to sell, and that is a legend. And he sells the legend with supreme skill, and despises the buyers. But there is another side to the bargain, and the playboy of the glens and islands is only just beginning to understand that he has sold himself with the legend. The world envies him and his past and makes every allowance for his temperament, but the world also has taken his land and destroyed his traditions. He will survive on new lands and with new traditions overseas, and will exert from Lake Ontario an influence upon the affairs of the Empire which he never exerted from the Linnhe Loch. But Lochaber is no more because the men of Lochaber have gone away. They have thrown their hand in and gracefully taken their leave, and left a dead land behind them. The emigrant ships which cruised so hopefully, and so successfully, around the islands of the Hebrides carried away more than men and women and children. They carried away Lochaber itself. There was no rearguard action. There was no stubbornness in defence. There was no heroism for a lost cause. The cause was lost from the first moment that the spirit of attack faltered. The Gael had shown himself from first to last to be strong in attack and graceful in retreat. And that is why he is eternally doomed to be the play-boy of the English, who are pertinacious in attack and stubborn in retreat. Where the Highlander bows elegantly, and flings a towel into the ring, the Englishman digs a trench and mans it until the crack of doom. The Highlander throughout history has won the first battle in each campaign and no more. The Englishman has won the last and no more.

The Highlander knows all this. He knows that he is a member of a dying race, and so he is a fatalist.

In two or three or four generations there will be no Highlanders left on the other side of the Line and the spirit of the Isles and the glens will only survive in the New World, so he finds it difficult to worry about anything very much. The kilt will be officially fancy-dress, the Aboyne Games will have the music, England will have the rest of the forests and moors which she does not yet have. The Gaelic Celt of the north who is the descendant partly of the Scottish Gael and the Irish Gael, and who is the inheritor of the gift of Columba, and, in some few parts, still the stubborn holder of the gift of Columba, will be inextricably confused with the Cymric Celt of the south. All will be classified, simply, as Scotch. We will all be described as "dour," as lacking in sense of humour, as keen businessmen, as enthusiastic admirers of Burns, as parsimonious, as ideal material for the manufacture of bank clerks.

So what does it matter?

The race in Scotland is dying. Contact with the English and their vigorous, vital ideas of progress, has sapped the Gael from strength to anaemia in less than two hundred years. Columba landed in 563, and for nearly twelve hundred years the glens withstood the social influences, the political theories, and the armed forces of the outer world. But the space from Culloden to the sheep-clearances, and from the sheep-clearances to the making of the deer-forests, and from the making of the deer-forests to the present day, is less than two centuries. That is all the little space of time that was needed for the killing of a race. English penetration, pressing relentlessly forward, has been as deadly as the germ of influenza has been to Polynesian or the common cold to Red Indian.

But in Canada the ancient spirit has room in which to breathe. Whitehall is blessedly far from Ontario, and the Highland race is as strong and as flourishing in Canada as it has ever been. But it will never return to the glens and the straths. It will only be in dreams that the Canadian Highlanders will see the Hebrides, however strong the blood and however Highland the heart. And it is right that this should be so. Lochaber, and all that it once stood for, is finished. Nothing can save it now. Still less can anything restore it. There is too much old sorrow, too much old bitterness, and too many old defeats. A more stubborn race might have redeemed the defeats. A more materially successful race might forget the bitterness. A more prosaic race might never have known the sorrow. But the Gael is none of these things. His race is dying in Scotland. Let it die. His land is being steadily turned into a large playground for the alien. Let it go. It is half-way there already. Let the other half follow. Soon nothing will be left of a proud race of soldiers and poets and musicians except descendants in the New World, and some pipe-music, and the memory, already fading fast, of some battles, and some romance, and some loyalties, and an infinite deal of sadness.

CHAPTER VII

Violence and Chicane in Lowland Scotland

I have tried to show how the Gaelic Celt has been no match for the Anglo-Saxon; how he has wilted at every contact; how he tried to begin as a conqueror and very soon ended as a play-boy; how he has lost everything in the short struggle except the wonderful rebirth of his race in Canada.

I am now going to talk about the Lowlander, whom Professor Windisch and Dr Whitley Stokes call the Cymric Celt, and to consider the impact of the Anglo-Saxon upon him. For it is obvious to anyone who agrees with what I have written in the first part of this book that, if there is any future hope of a Scottish Renaissance, it will not come from the Highlands. That is an idea which must be dismissed at once. Culloden was more than the end of the ambitions of Charles Edward. It was the complete, rounded, perfect illustration of what happens when the Scottish Gael in mass meets the Anglo-Saxon in mass. Children, however brave, however gaily dressed, however vain, can never make a great showing against grown men.

So if there is any hope for the continuance of what may be called, not so much Scotland — which is only a geographical or ethnological term — but "the idea of Scotland" — which is the soul of the country — it must lie in the Lowlands. The Highlanders are not a broken reed, but a bending reed, which is much worse. A broken reed must have put up a stout resistance, otherwise it could not have been broken. The story of Scotland must be, in fact, the reverse of the Psalmist who lifted up his eyes to the hills for his help. The only help lies in the plains. That is where the strength of Scotland is, and that is where the strength of Scotland, for good or for evil, has been for many a year.

* * *

In the years before Edward the First, the Lowlander had had a strong tendency towards friendship with the English. The refugees, as I have said, who came north after William the First had conquered England, were well received by the Scots, and later, the Norman adventurers, who were not content, as Normans have never been content, with the dull life at home, also got a warm welcome. With these refugees and adventurers came the new ideas from France, of which the castle, cavalry, and the feudal system were the most important. These were the three weapons with which the Lowlanders defended themselves on the two strategical fronts which they had to man.

The feeling of friendship towards the English was all changed by Edward. It was Edward who created the great barrier between the nations, and although he has gone down to posterity as the Hammer of the Scots, nevertheless the only thing which he hammered out upon his anvil was the iron determination of the Lowland Scot to be independent of England. But it was a cruel and a bloody smithy, and in those wars, which were the direct result of Edward Plantagenet's ambitions, Scotland suffered appalling miseries.

This was the crucial era for the Lowlander, for it made him what he is. This was the key-period. The citizen of today is descended from 1292, not from Alexander the Third or Queen Margaret. All through these early wars there are three distinct notes, which are repeated over and over again. The very same notes are repeated in every later war in which the Lowlander has taken part. They are even in some measure repeated in almost every aspect of the Lowland genius. They are the heroism of the common soldiers; the stupidity, after the great age of the Bruce-Douglas-Randolph partnership, of the leaders; and the indomitability of the people.

The Scots were defeated over and over again, disastrously, in major battles. Dupplin, Halidon Hill, Nevill's Cross, Homildon Hill, Flodden, Solway Moss, Pinkie, all were overwhelming English victories. Any one of them would have smashed the Highlands to pieces. But the Lowlander came up resiliently after each of them, and was just as determined to preserve his independence after the last as he had been before the first. His ally at Bannockburn, the Gaelic clans, had retired into the hills. But the plainsman went on with the defence of the country.

* * *

Edward the First left another legacy behind him that has stamped itself even more deeply into the Lowland character than courage and indomitability in low places, or stupidity in high. The best way to appreciate this legacy will be to turn aside for a moment and consider the "Auld Alliance" between Scotland and France.

By a curious irony it was friendship for England which first brought French influence into Scotland, and hatred for England which brought it into Scotland for a second time. The Norman adventurers were welcome because they came from England. The French Alliance was welcome because after 1292 it was directed against England.

In the fourteenth century both Scotland and France were fighting for their lives against the English archers, and it was inevitable that they should come together for mutual defence and, when the opportunity presented itself, for concerted aggression.

France gained from the Alliance a useful little military ally. Scotland certainly gained a powerful military ally and the advantage of coming into contact with culture and the civilised arts. But unquestionably there were disadvantages as well. It was the vehement pressure of the French, for example, which induced King David to march to Nevill's Cross in 1346, and although it was very pleasant for poor Scottish nobles to visit the fair land of France as honoured guests and allies, the pleasure was much diminished when they were led into such affairs as the disaster at Verneuil in 1424, when the stupidity of the Comte de Narbonne led to the destruction of the Scottish contingent and the deaths of the Earls of Douglas and of Buchan, of Home of Wedderburn, Swinton, Lindsay, and many another Border gentleman.

Again, in the fifteenth century the French were using the Avignon captivity of the Popes as a weapon in their political manoeuvres, and Scotland had to toe the Avignonese line on the instructions of their senior partner. The recognition of the anti-Popes on the orders of a foreign power, however friendly, for political purposes, could not fail to damage the spiritual unity of a Catholic country.

As for the cultural advantages to be derived from a close friendship with the country of Abelard and Villon, and the Pleiade, and the early flowering of the French Renaissance, the seeds of the liberal arts have seldom been sown upon stonier ground. The history of the medieval Lowlands is one long record of barbarity, savagery, and treachery. North of the Highland Line there may have been barbarity and savagery among the clans. But the essence of the clan-system lay in loyalty. The men of each clan were loyal not only to their Chiefs, but also to the men of friendly clans. But south of the Line, where French culture had an opportunity of spreading some sort of sense of decency, and where the soft French wines of Bordeaux were already driving out the harsh usquebaugh of the natives, treachery was the everyday practice of the great feudal lords. Each man fought for his own hand, and fought with abominable weapons. Brothers stabbed brothers, friends starved friends to death in dungeons, fathers hired assassins to murder sons, and sons betrayed fathers to their enemies. The great names of Douglas and Albany, Mar and Boyd and Colville and Hamilton, are for the most part simply the names of treacherous murderers. And on one of the rare occasions when a man of culture, King James the Third, might have influenced the country, he was brutally murdered at Beaton's Mill by an adherent of the Homes and Hepburns, who had revolted against the royal authority. Violence and chicane were more powerful in Lowland Scotland than any of the liberal arts.

But why was this? Why had an apparently civilised country, in close alliance, politically and socially, with the sweet land of France, sunk into this dreadful morass of barbarity? And it was worse than barbarity. The cannibal king who states openly and frankly that he intends to chop into small pieces, fry, and eat, any missionary upon whom he can lay his hands, is a comparatively decent and honest fellow. He does not mince matters, whatever he may do to the missionary. He does not betray him. He does not deceive him. He makes no bones, so to speak, about his intention. But the medieval Lowlander was a horrible scoundrel in comparison with a frank and open-hearted cannibal chief. He was treacherous as well as savage, dishonourable as well as brutal.

The reason is well set out by Mr Eric Linklater in his *The Lion and the Unicorn*.

"It may be said," writes Mr Linklater, "without possibility of contradiction, that Scotland had been forced into its conception of patriotism-as-hatred by the destruction policy of Edward I."

That is the first point that must be grasped in estimating the Lowland character. It was founded upon Hate. The rich, fatly-equipped, professional armies of Edward Plantagenet swamped the poor levies of a poor country. The lands; for the most part unfertile in times of peace, were harried into a desert in time of English war. Churches, abbeys, houses, hovels, were destroyed. And, worst of all, and sowing the most fatal seeds of all, Scotsmen were turned against Scotsmen. Edward made John Baliol King of Scotland and began the hatred of brother against brother, just as he founded the hatred of Lowlander for Englishman.

"Hatred was of Edward's making," writes Mr Linklater. "When Alexander died, Scotland was a land of busy and various interests, happy in its prosperity, and eager for culture. When Edward died it was poor and bloody and desperate, a land with one determination, to live in despite of England, and with one luxury, hatred of England."

So the tale of the Lowlands begins from 1292 with this ever-gathering, ever-increasing flood of hatred. A comparatively peaceful country had been turned into a country of semi-independent, semi-savage banditti. And the hatred inevitably turned inwards as well as outwards. That is to say, after a time it was not only the English who were hated and feared and distrusted. Each one of the leaders of the banditti was hated and feared and distrusted by the rest. Neighbour distrusted, and was ready to hate, neighbour. Noble was only too ready to hate noble. Factions sprang up on every hand, all animated by the legacy of Edward the Hammer, and all using the only weapon they understood, the weapon bequeathed to them by Edward, violence.

The feudal families of the south had been turned into fierce and ruthless soldiers by the English wars. Not only that, but the families which stood out pre-eminent as fiercer and more ruthless than the rest, inevitably gained power in the affairs of not only their neighbours but of the State. Where violence was the order of the day, a man who could rely on a couple of hundred men-at-arms, mounted if possible, was a more valuable ally, not only in the field but in the council-chamber, than the man who could only muster one hundred men-at-arms. Then, as must always happen in war, industry, commerce, finance, or statecraft, whenever one or two or three individuals or entities rise above the common ruck, they rise higher still and the rest sink lower. The prudent and the cowardly — and what is called in modern politics "the floating vote" — naturally gravitate towards the strong, so that the strong become stronger all the time, and the weak weaker. In modern industry the process is identical and is called merger, combine, or trust.

This is what happened in medieval Scotland. A few families such as Douglas, Murray, Scott, Hamilton, became so powerful that they could, and did, challenge the authority of the King himself. Indeed it was fortunate for the royal house that the handful of families which had grasped the elementary principles of the modern merger, had not the intelligence, or perhaps the good-will, to carry the principle to its modern and logical end and combine into one big monopoly of fighting-power. But this they never approached. The legacy of hate which Edward Plantagenet had bequeathed to them enabled them to hate each other just as savagely as they had ever hated the English, and they came to regard the monarchy not as an enemy, nor as an object of personal ambition, and certainly not as a thing to be destroyed, but rather as a fixed point round which to manoeuvre — to use Napoleon's words — against rival murderers and scoundrels. Each of the great families was so anxious to prevent all the others from attaining the monarchy that they preferred to leave it as an institution permanently in the hands of the Stuarts.

* * *

The internal history of South Scotland during the fifteenth century, and especially during the reigns of the first three James's, is one long tale of barbarism in high places. And we must not forget that this was the century in which the Renaissance was advancing to its full bloom in Europe. Scotland, the country of St Margaret and Alexander the Third, which had enjoyed a thirteenth century of peace, civilisation, and prestige, was reduced in the flowering fifteenth to the cultural and moral level of a Balkan province under Turkish domination.

The hammer of Edward was still ringing upon the anvil.

At the beginning of the sixteenth century a deadly blow was struck at the murderous barons of the Lowlands, a blow from which they never recovered. As foolish in pitched battle as they were brave in individual combat, the aristocracy of Scotland was almost annihilated at Flodden in 1513. It was, of course, entirely their own fault. The Scottish tactics at Flodden were grotesque in their folly. The only quality on which the Scottish aristocracy could pride itself was its military capacity, and at Flodden they showed that even in this quality they were completely negligible. The Earl of Surrey violated every rule of strategy when he made his flank-march, and at any moment during the march he might have been destroyed. But he was obviously a good psychologist, and knew the sort of people he was fighting against. With a more skilful opponent the flank-march must have ended in disaster, but with a more skilful opponent he would not have attempted it. The Duke of Wellington, in the Peninsula, varied his tactics and tempered his audacity according to the French Marshal against him. The Earl of Surrey obviously did the same at Flodden. He knew that he was confronted by a foolish and a vain set of aristocrats. Their folly and their vanity brought Scotland's brief renaissance to the ground.

Fifteen years of chaos followed, and then James the Fifth completed the ruin of the barons which had been almost achieved by the English at Flodden, by a series of unexpected, ruthless, treacherous, and entirely justifiable executions, both in the Highlands and the Lowlands.

The royal hanging of such men as Piers Cockburn of Henderland, Adam Scott of Tushielaw, and John Armstrong of Gilnockie, was almost the last manifestation of the first phase of Edward's legacy of hatred and violence. The sequence of horror ran true and unbroken from the day in November, 1292, when John Baliol did homage to a Plantagenet, up to the hanging of John Armstrong, in 1529. The hatred during these two and a half centuries was political, and the violence was political.

But now the wheel took a new and even grimmer turn.

CHAPTER VIII

The Reformation and Calvin

So far we have reached the following position. An independent nation, after enjoying a century of years in the way in which it wanted to live, in peace and goodwill, has been brutally compelled, by outside compulsion, to fight for its life. After that fight is over, more or less, the habit remains, and a brutalised nation faces whatever the world has to offer it. And what the world has to offer it is, suddenly and dramatically, the greatest revolution which the Christian world has yet known. At noon on All Saints' Day, 1513, Luther nailed his Ninety-five Theses to the door of the Castle Church of Wittenberg. It was the beginning of the second phase of hatred and violence in Scotland.

In this second phase, the bitterness turned from politics to religion. But, and this is the vitally important point, the second phase came from England just as the first phase had come from England. Luther lit the spark, but it was Henry the Eighth who sent the resulting torch into the north.

At first the new Reforming ideas were coldly received, not because they were Reforming, but because they came from England. There was still enough of the spirit of Bruce alive in the Lowlands to distrust and dislike anything that came from England. The Catholic Church in Scotland was rank with corruption and abuse. But it was, at first at any rate, still preferable to anything which came out of England.

"In this poor and sparsely peopled country," says F. W. Maitland, "the church was wealthy; the clergy were numerous, laic, and lazy. The names of 'dumb dogs' and 'idle Bellies' which the new preachers fixed upon them had not been unearned. Nowhere else was there a seed-plot better prepared for revolutionary ideas of a religious sort. Nowhere else would an intelligible Bible be a newer book, or a sermon kindle stranger fires. Nowhere else would the pious champions of the Catholic Faith be compelled to say so much that was evil of those who should have been their pastors."

But in spite of this state of affairs in a land that was blackened by civil wars and ruined by foreign wars, the English-exported Reformation was, at first, coldly received. But a dynasty was on the throne of England that was as powerful and as ruthless and as self-willed as the Plantagenets. The Tudors were afraid of nothing, Spain, Scotland, Rome, or God. They understood, as no dynasty of English monarchs has ever so clearly understood, that the soul of England can only be preserved on the sea. Henry the Seventh began to build a navy, and Henry the Eighth completed the weapon which his daughter used so triumphantly. With this weapon the Tudors could snap their fingers at the world. And they did.

When Henry the Eighth, secure behind the ships of the new model which Hawkins was building for him, broke with Rome, he was determined not to allow Catholic Scotland to march with his Protestant England. And so the Reformation had to go north.

If the Scots would not be annexed by fair means, they must be harried by foul, and once again the Englishry invaded and burnt and sacked. The Scottish aristocracy was thus given another opportunity for double-dealing and treachery. Some fought on one side, some on the other, none for Scotland, and all for self-interest.

But what could not be forced upon Scotland by armies, even by armies that were so overwhelmingly victorious as the Protector Somerset's at Pinkie in 1547, could be forced upon her in other ways.

The great Cardinal Beaton was one of the obstacles in the English path of Church reformation, and so he was removed by murder. It need hardly be said that the murderers who removed Scotland's champion from England's path were not English. A Leslie, a Melville, Kirkcaldy of Grange, and the Master of Rothes, Scots aristocrats all, did the work for a wage of £1180, paid by Henry the Eighth. This was at St Andrews. The murderers, with a crew of drunken friends, paid by England, held St Andrews and enjoyed a brief career of debauchery. But they were not so lost in their revels that they forgot all sense of political expediency. Their paymaster was the English king, and he had abjured "Papery, and idolatry, and image-worship and surplices, and sic like rags o' the muckle hure that sitteth on seven hills," so they, in the intervals of assassination and debauchery, went occasionally to church to hear the new "gospel." The preacher was John Knox.

The chain of fatality unwinds itself. Each link leads inevitably to the next link. There is no pause and no hesitation and no flaw. That which started with Edward's hammer has now reached, inevitably, to the sermons of Knox and to the Scotsmen who murdered Scotland's great Cardinal.

The story is not nearly half-way through.

Hatred and violence are now in their full stride in this new direction.

The Reforming party in England had seized the monasteries. Henry would have kept the loot in his own hands, but the looting nobles, landowners, and new merchant class compelled him to give up almost all of it, and a new capitalist class, recruited to a certain extent from what we would now call the middle class, but mainly from the fighting aristocracy, came into existence.

The repercussion on Scotland was quick and clear. There were monasteries in Scotland too. There was a fighting aristocracy, poorer, more pugnacious, and much less honourable, than its corresponding level in English society. And there was a steady pressure, military, economic, and social, from the Tudor court upon the Stuart court, to adopt the new religion.

It is hardly surprising that the wretched kingdom of Scotland succumbed to the double pressure of pikemen from without and greed from within, and the Reformation burst with a fearful ferocity in 1559, and the zeal which had hitherto gone to the hacking off of political heads now turned towards the destruction of beautiful buildings and the harrying of Papists. Knox brought with him "the Book of Geneva," and the Calvinian brand of Protestantism became the fixed standard of worship for the Scottish Church. This, again, is an interesting and characteristic point. The Lowlander, after two and a half centuries of struggle against the English, accepted Protestantism as a general principle partly at the persuasion and partly on the peremptory orders of the English. But he tried to salve his national conscience and to assert, at a belated hour, his intellectual independence by striking out a new side-line of his own and taking Calvinism from a Frenchman in Geneva instead of Lutheranism from London. Perhaps it is too complimentary to the subconscious independence of the Lowlander to say that he deliberately chose Calvinism. It may have been chance that the forceful, cowardly personality of John Knox happened to be in the popular eye at the critical moment. Or it may have been that the blackest and most dismal variant of Protestantism appealed most strongly to a nation that had been compelled, by external pressure and internal villainy, to become bleak and dismal itself.

But whatever the cause, the historical fact is there. The Lowlands of Scotland sprang with a hungry avidity upon the doctrines of Calvin.

And having got these doctrines, the Lowlands of Scotland proceeded to treat the religious situation, which had come to it indirectly from England, exactly as it had in the past treated the political situation, which had also come to it from England.

That is to say, by hatred and violence.

It is unnecessary to linger on the atrocities which were committed on both sides, on the fanatical deadliness of the struggle, or on the gloomy dogmatics which soon took and held the place which religion had once held. The genius of the Lowlander found itself instinctively as much at home with a new bell, book, and candle, as it had ever found itself with the old two-handed sword. The national individualism of the race and the natural stubborn refusal to bow to tyranny were given full scope by the Calvinian Reformation. But it would be a mistake to write down the theological fervour of the Lowlander, his disputatiousness, his stern, unbending refusal to accept compromise in religious quarrels, his puritanical narrow-mindedness, and, of course, his Sabbath-Day observance, as the direct result of Calvinism. The gloomy French-Genevese did not mould the Lowland character. He found it already moulded by the English wars. All he did was to give a religious twist to the existing dismalness, stubbornness, and fanaticism. The story is not episodic. It is continuous.

We now come to the second vitally important date in Scottish history, the year in which Elizabeth died and the road to the rich south was thrown open for the first time. It was a wonderful stroke of luck, and the hungry, poverty-stricken, uncouth folk of the north were not by any means backward in taking advantage of it. They swarmed into London and jostled each other and the English, in the race for wealth and position. It was only natural that James should give a considerable amount of preferment to those who had served him in humbler circumstances, and it was only natural that the English should resent the rapid promotion of the needy and pushing barbarians whom they had so often defeated upon the field of pitched battle. The marauders who had never managed by war to penetrate south of Durham, had penetrated by peace into the very heart of London, and appeared to regard it in very much the same way as their fathers had regarded the rich abbeys of Northumberland, as a pretty place to sack. It was some time before the English lost their first keen resentment and settled down to their age-old trick of assimilation. How they ultimately devised that process of assimilation, and how they absorbed the Scottish invasion, will appear later in this book.

At first the English were completely puzzled and resentful at the Scottish invasion. Nor is this surprising. The family which came south to sit upon the throne of the Tudors, arrived from the Lowland capital, Edinburgh, and was brought down by its Lowland connections and supported by its Lowland power, and yet it was a Highland family. It is no wonder that the English could not understand the Stuarts. In the first place the Stuarts were brilliant intellectually. The four Stuart kings were perhaps the most enlightened, the most intelligent and the best educated kings who have ever reigned in England. But, in the second place, their trouble was that three of them, Charles II being the exception, were too clever by half. The three never understood the English character. Paradoxically it would be equally true to say that these three were the only English kings who were clever enough to understand the English character perfectly. The Stuarts were clever enough to see that the English are the cleverest race in the world, and so the English hated them. It is and always has been the main asset in the shop window of the English that they are a stupid race, and it is this asset which has taken them triumphantly all over the world. The Stuarts tried to tackle this cleverness with their own, and the result was their inevitable overthrow. On two occasions the English had opportunities of getting rid of this brilliant Highland family, and they seized both. On the first occasion they chopped off the head of the King in order to make room for a Midland squire of a Welsh family, and on the second occasion they threw out the King to make room for a dull and heavy Dutchman and a string of even duller and heavier Germans.

But if the English disliked and distrusted the Stuart kings, still more did they dislike and distrust the courtiers who came south in the first half of the seventeenth century. The contemporary writings of the Southerners are full of reference to the proud, poverty-stricken hangers-on who forced their way into London.

It is not surprising that the Scots who came south, already suffering from the wars and the defeats of the past, should have detested the superior and often arrogant behaviour of the English.

This feeling of mutual dislike may not have been aggravated by the founding in 1608 of the Blackheath Golf Club, but it certainly was by the Civil War and rising of the English middle class against the Scottish King. The patriotic Lowlander was torn between two intense emotions. Firstly, he detested with all his dark and violent heart the English who wanted to expel, or at any rate to defeat, the Stuart. That was an insult to Scotland, sufficient to rouse the whole country south of the Highland Line. On the other hand there was an even stronger passion raging in the Lowlands, and that was the hatred of Catholicism. So, to the Scot, the Civil War was at once a disaster and a triumph, and the Scots decided in the end to join in on the side of the triumph.

It is, however, unjust to say, as so many have said, that in 1647 they sold the King to the English. The money which they received was due to them by the English Parliament, and it was simply an unfortunate coincidence that they handed over Charles the First at the precise moment that they received the first instalment of their money.

They handed over the King not for cash but because he refused the terms which they offered him in return for their support in the field.

A year or two later they changed their mind and once again engaged the English in a pitched battle, and once again they displayed the stupidity which is, as we have seen, characteristic of the Lowland commander in almost every first-class battle since Bannockburn. Having manoeuvred Cromwell into a trap at Dunbar, the military commanders allowed the fanatical preachers to dictate the tactics, and the natural result was an overwhelming disaster. The battle of Dunbar is an interesting detail in the story, as it shows several angles of the Lowland character.

There was firstly the unshakeable courage. And here it must be remembered that the Scottish army was perfectly confident in its own bravery and determination in the face of Cromwell, the greatest soldier in Britain. Secondly, there was the characteristic doggedness with which the Scots had collected the army and brought it to the critical point in the campaign. Thirdly, there was the insanity of tactics which has always ruined their strategy. And, fourthly, there was the dominance of the preachers over the soldiers. Everything was subordinated, the lives of the rank and file, the safety of the country and the cause of the monarchy, to the claims of theology. This fourth point is an illuminating one as it illustrates perfectly the change in the Lowland outlook which had been wrought by the Reformation. The hatred and violence had been turned from military affairs to theology to such an extent that even in the face of the enemy, and that the ancient hereditary enemy, the old fighting instinct was dominated by the new preaching instinct. Alexander Leslie was a skilful and veteran soldier, but even he could not resist the claims of ecclesiastics to control the hazard of battle in the face of Oliver Cromwell.

CHAPTER IX

Scots in the Army, Navy and Empire

The battle of Dunbar, in which Cromwell had to match his wits and military talents against those of the Covenanting preachers, was the last occasion on which the descendants of the Douglas fought a battle against the descendants of the Percy. It was the last of the long series. The Highlanders had still to make their two raids into England, to Worcester and to Derby, but for the Lowlander the warfare was finished. I think, then, that this is the moment at which to say a word about the subsequent military connection between the Lowlands and England. Chronologically, the beginning of this connection is at this very period — the middle of the seventeenth century — but the story itself, if it is to be begun at all, must be carried at least as far as Haig. But although this means a certain dislocation in the continuity which I am trying to maintain, it is necessary to endure it at this point because the foundation of the Royal Scots in 1662 is a notable event in the relations between the Lowlander and the Englishman. After this chapter I will return to the main stream of continuity where we left it — that is to say, the second half of the seventeenth century.

For at least five hundred years Scottish adventurers went abroad in search of fame and fortune and position. Some tried to achieve their ambition as administrators, notably in the Baltic region, some, like Law of Lauriston, as financiers, a few as sailors like that Russian Admiral, Samuel Greig, who is buried in Reval cathedral, but the great majority of them as soldiers. There was a steady flow of professional military talent for centuries, and the names of Scottish soldiers are strewn across the campaigns of every European country from the Pas de Calais to Constantinople and from the Marches of Portugal to the Ural mountains.

The classic example in fiction is, of course, Sir Dugald Dalgetty in Scott's *The Legend of Montrose.*

The classic example in history is James Keith, the second son of an eighteenth-century Earl Marischal of Scotland. Realising as a young man in the early twenties that the only hope of advancement for the second son of an aristocratic family depended entirely upon his own head and his own right arm, young Keith went abroad and served with the Spanish armies in the siege of Gibraltar in 1726. His efficient and energetic Scottish soul soon revolted, however, against the incompetence, the laziness, and the stupidity of the Spanish, and he accepted with eagerness an invitation to serve in the Russian armies. His career in Russia was spectacular. The Empress Anne formed such a high opinion of his talents, and perhaps an even higher opinion of his fidelity and incorruptibility, that she suddenly promoted him, although he could hardly speak a word of Russian, to the command of the Moscow Garrison when she left the old capital to take up residence in Petersburg.

Keith was so successful and so tactful in the difficult position in which he was placed that in the following year the Empress promoted him to one of the three new Inspector-Generalships of the Army. Thenceforward his fortunes steadily rose. Post after post was given to him and honours were poured upon him. He became successively Governor of the Ukraine, Lieutenant-General in the Army, Governor of Finland, Minister-Plenipotentiary in Sweden, Minister and Commander of the Armies against the Turks. But all his efficiency and all his tact could not prevent the native Russians from becoming jealous of the foreigner and the favours the Empress showed him. And finally, in disgust at the political intrigues, Keith resigned all his appointments and left Russia for ever.

In any other age or with a man of any other nationality than Scottish, this might well have been the conclusion of a remarkable career. With Keith it was only the end of an episode.

Within a few weeks after leaving Russia, he was a Field-Marshal in the service of Frederick the Great, and fought in the Seven Years' War as the trusted friend, adviser and right-hand man of the Prussian king. He fell in action at the Battle of Hochkirch, and Frederick put up a statue to him in Berlin and named an infantry regiment after him.

In all the long history of the soldiers who left Scotland to take service abroad, perhaps the most curious example is to be found in the Peninsular War. During the campaign in Catalonia in 1810 a Spanish army, in the field against the French, was commanded by an Irishman, Henry O'Donnell. He was opposed by a mixed army of French and Italians commanded by a Scotsman, Etienne Macdonald. There have, of course, been many occasions, notably in the Turkish wars, when roving Scotsmen fought on both sides, but the Catalonian campaign of 1810 is the only example I know in which a member of the ancient Gaelic house of Donald commanded on each side.

The Scots always took a professional interest in the trade of warfare, and studied almost every angle of it with native thoroughness. I say "almost," because there were curious gaps in their studies, the most notable of which were the use of the long-bow and the principles of generalship. But on the whole they displayed for centuries a great aptitude for warfare and for its details. Dr J. M. Bulloch has pointed out that, for an example, one small part of Scotland, the rural and fishing district north of Aberdeen which is called Buchan, has made no less than four distinctive contributions to the details of warfare. James Keith himself, who was born at Inverugie near Peterhead, invented the Kriegsschachspiel or War-Game. Colonel Patrick Ferguson (1744-1780) from Pitfour invented the breech-loading rifle. The Rev. Alexander John Forsyth (1769-1843), the Minister of Belhelvie, invented the percussion lock, and General Sir Harry Burnett Lumsden (1821-1896), the Laird of Belhelvie, invented khaki. In passing, on the subject of the percussion lock, it is interesting to note that Forsyth took his invention to the authorities in London who threw him and his "trash" out contemptuously, and that the Duke of Wellington refused to have anything to do with the new invention, infinitely preferring his own clumsy muzzle-loading musket. The attitude of English commanders towards new-fangled weapons has been the same down the ages, from the days when the chivalry of the later Plantagenets regarded the use of gunpowder as unsporting to the later days when the products of the Staff Colleges at Camberley and Quetta fought so hard, and for a long time so successfully, against the use of machine-guns and tanks.

The foundation of the Royal Scots in 1662 was the first organized attempt by England to divert this flow of mercenary talent for warfare from the Continent to her own service.

It was so successful a beginning that it was soon followed by others. The Royal Scots Fusiliers was founded in 1677 and was recruited in Glasgow and Ayrshire. In 1689 came the King's Own Scottish Borderers, based on the five Border counties and wearing trousers of Leslie tartan. It was a Scottish regiment, but its headquarters were in the English city of Berwick-on-Tweed. In the same year there was a remarkable event — the raising of the Cameronians in the region round Hamilton. What made this new regiment's birth so remarkable was that for the first time in history the colours of Douglas, for that is the tartan of which the trousers of the Cameronians are made, were worn in the service of a King reigning south of the border.

The usual assimilative spells of the English were quickly at work. These new regiments were soon fighting heroically at Namur and Blenheim, and by the time that the Prince had landed in Moidart their sympathies were entirely on the side of the Hanoverians. Even the Black Watch, which as I have said was originally composed mainly of men from Jacobite and Catholic clans, had so far altered in character and outlook that it fought under Johnny Cope at Prestonpans and was cut to pieces for its pains. A company of the Royal Scots ran away from the battle of Falkirk, but avenged themselves under Cumberland at Culloden.

It is interesting to note that both these regiments had become so anglicised in outlook that neither the Royal Scots nor the Black Watch seemed to notice anything incongruous, or perhaps tragic is the fitter word, in the tartan worn by the soldiers of the one or the pipers of the other. For the soldiers wore, and still wear, the Hunting Stuart, the pipers wear the Royal Stuart.

The Gordon Highlanders were raised in 1794 by Alexander, Fourth Duke of Gordon. His main object was apparently to rid his family of the suspicion that they were adherents of the Jacobite cause. This was a most ingenious device. In order to prove that neither he nor his clan were concerned in the aspirations of the Highlanders, he formed a regiment to serve in the English army and actually called it by the very name from which he was desperately trying to disassociate himself. Passionately anxious not to be associated with the Highlands, he called his regiment, which after all was recruited from a Lowland district and from a Border clan, the Gordon Highlanders. The regiment is based at Aberdeen. But although neither the clan nor the district were Highland, nevertheless the new regiment attracted a number of recruits from the west, 245 coming from Inverness, 33 from Argyll, 20 from Ross, and 14 from Sutherland. Indeed, while there were 39 MacDonalds, 35 Macphersons, 35 Camerons and 18 Stewarts, there were only 16 Gordons in it.

With the formation of these line regiments, and the Scots Greys, the flow of talent to the Continent dried to a steadily decreasing trickle. There were still many Highlanders abroad, especially now that the Stuart kings were in exile, but when Pitt created the Highland regiments that tributary dried up also, and the flow ceased altogether. England had gently but inevitably gathered all the waters together into her own reservoir. It had taken her almost exactly a hundred years. What is a hundred years to England?

* * *

It was often useful for recruiting purposes to make a clan-chief into a colonel at once, or to start one of the lesser chieftains as a major. That was a reasonable method of attracting the clansmen. But there was no intention of promoting the majors or colonels into the generalship. The newcomers had to work their way up the last rungs of the ladder of promotion by seniority just like anyone else. There were no short cuts to a Field-Marshal's baton such as Frederick the Great opened to Keith. Thus in the war against France in Canada many splendid feats of arms were performed by the new Highland regiments, but the Commander at Quebec was Wolfe, who was born in a country vicarage in Kent; a man who not merely disliked all Scots, but who had taken an active part in 1746 in Cumberland's atrocities in the glens. In the American

1. Bridge of Balgownie. Bruce marched across it.

2. Bridge at Stirling. Wallace fought here.

3. Inveraray. Home of the Clan Campbell.

4. Glencoe.

Right: 5. Highlanders of Chatham's Regiments.

Below: 6. Highlanders of General Harper's Regiments.

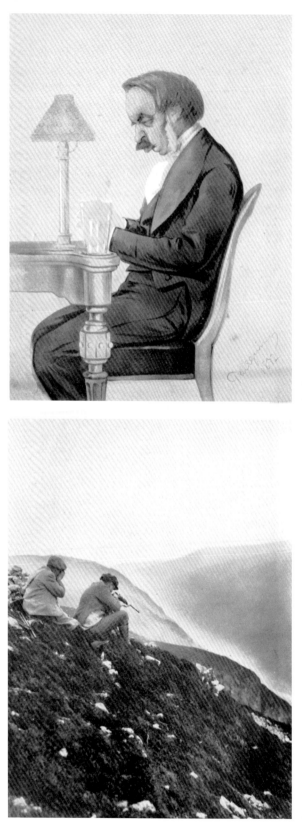

7. Mr Mackenzie of Kintail. A highland chief, 1872.

8. An English sportsman.

Right: 9. Dancing for the tourist.

Below: 10. Tossing the caber for the tourist.

11. Loch Coruisk, Skye.

12. The Kyle of Loch Alsh.

13. Little Vermilion Lake, Ontario.

14. Parliament Building, Ottawa.

15. Elgin Cathedral, after John Knox.

16. Iona, the Holy Island.

Above: 17. Calcutta, centre of the jute industry.

Right: 18. The Bank of England.

Above: 19. Pittsburg, the birthplace of Scotland Free Libraries.

Left: 20. Carnegie Free Library, Dunfermline.

21. The Glasgow engineer at work.

22. The finished article.

Above: 23. Old Scotland.

Left: 24. New Scotland.

Right: 25. Mr R. T. Jones, of Atlanta, Georgia.

Below: 26. Scotland v. England, at Hampden Park, Glasgow.

27. An alleged type.

28. More alleged types.

Left: 29. Edinburgh Castle.

Below: 30. Holyrood.

War of Independence there were Highlanders in the United Empire Loyalists, but the Commanders were Burgoyne, Cornwallis, and Howe; the decisive commanders against Napoleon were Nelson and Wellington, and the only Scotsman who held command in the Napoleonic wars is mainly distinguished for having fallen in action at Corunna after conducting one of the fastest and most incompetent retreats on record. It was an English Admiral, Codrington, who commanded at Navarino in 1827, and an Englishman who commanded in the Crimea.

Indeed it is not until we come to the Indian wars, a hundred years and more after the rising of 1745, that we find more than an occasional Scotsman in command of British armies. Even then the imagination is apt to be coloured by the sound of the bagpipes going through the streets of Lucknow to the Residency, so that one forgets that the handful of men who really saved India during the Mutiny were the young Englishmen in the Punjab, and not the Scottish soldiers like Sir Colin Campbell and Sir James Outram.

In the Boer War the outstanding figures were Roberts and Kitchener. Hector Macdonald caught the public imagination, as Highlanders are apt to do. But he was not a great soldier or anywhere near it.

The World War of 1914-1918 was the one notable exception in that for the first time outside India a Scotsman was Commander-in-Chief of the main British army, the army on the Western Front. Another Scotsman, Murray, commanded the army in Palestine, and Hamilton and Munro at the Dardanelles, and Sir William Robertson was for a time Chief of the Imperial General Staff, and Sir Rosslyn Wemyss was First Sea Lord.

But in the main the senior generals of the World War were English or Irish; Plumer, Rawlinson, Byng, Gough, French, Allenby, Harington, Maude, Birdwood, and, of course, Jellicoe and Beatty on the High Seas. Of all those in the imperial forces who played high parts in the war only two were completely outstanding in talent, or if you prefer it, in genius — Jellicoe and T. E. Lawrence, and both were Englishmen.

It is obvious, therefore, that while England gained immensely from the services of Scotsmen in her armies, the Scots themselves were for a long time the losers. In the old centuries of free-lancing, often literally, on the Continent of Europe, the Scotsman might reach almost the highest post in any army within a week. After he turned his eyes to the lure of the Sassenach he found a safe career but a slow one. The romance and the profits were taken out of professional soldiering. England, closed one career to him and opened another and a duller one. In the first he tried to carve out a livelihood for himself; in the second he was set to carve out an empire for England. The world was still open to him but in very different conditions.

CHAPTER X

Darien and the Union

The closer contact with England which the Union of the Thrones had brought about, had a deep effect upon the trend of thought in the Lowlands. We have seen how the outbreak of the Reformation turned the national individualism and violence from militarism to theology; contact with the prosperous, mercantile England turned them from the consideration of the affairs of the next world to a consideration of the affairs of this.

It might not appear at first sight that a country which could allow, in 1650, its veteran army commander to be overruled by the preachers had gone very far along the road to materialism. But two events, both of which took place before the end of the century, within fifty years of Dunbar, proved that a new spirit was certainly moving.

The first was that the layman suddenly asserted himself in religious matters over the ministers of religion, a thing which had not happened since 1559, and declared Presbyterianism to be the national religion. And what is more, the reason why Presbyterianism was so established was not because it was right in the eyes of Heaven, as the ministers claimed, but because it was expedient for the country. Fifty years earlier such a thing would have been unheard of.

The second proof of the new spirit was the Darien venture. The wealth of England, seen at the new, closer range, had become very desirable to the needy north, and the dark violent character brooded over it jealously, until the desire for wealth had almost completely ousted dogmatics from the dark violent heart. The result was the Darien scheme. London was drawing riches from her fabulous East India Company. Why should not Edinburgh, from a fabulous Darien Company? England had her overseas trade. Why should not Scotland have hers?

The arguments were just, and the scheme might have proved sound. But London was not interested in the justice of arguments, and was resolved that the scheme should not be proved sound. So the merchants and financiers of London brought such pressure to bear upon the new Dutch King, upon

Parliament, upon financial circles, upon Hamburg, that they killed the Darien scheme dead and brought disaster upon Scotland.

Neither Glencoe nor Darien — coming within a few years of each other — might have seemed a good advertisement of the blessings of southern rule. But within another ten years England made proposals for an enormous extension of these blessings. Glencoe had lost its men, women, and children; the Darien investors had lost their money. Now Scotland was to lose its Parliament.

Up to the year 1707 Edinburgh was the capital of a country. It may have been a backward country, ravaged by external wars, distracted by internal wars, and smouldering with bitter religious animosities. But it was at least a country. The Union of the Parliaments changed all that.

The Edinburgh Parliament went south and the men of ambition went south with them. The Scottish centre of gravity, social, artistic, political, financial, and commercial, was transferred to London, and it has remained there ever since.

The Union came from London. And so it takes its place with Edward the First and the Reformation as the third of England's gifts. People may agree or disagree about the material advantages conferred upon Scotland by the Union. But there can be no disagreement about the methods by which the Union was forced through the Edinburgh Parliament. The people were strongly against the Union, and there were riots in Glasgow and Edinburgh, and even the Cameronians, who bitterly detested the Popish Jacobites, joined hands with their enemies to resist the destruction of the political independence of the country.

> "On the 23rd October," wrote Sir Walter Scott, "the popular fury was at its height. The people crowded together in the High Street and Parliament Square, and greeted their representatives as friends or enemies to their country, according as they opposed or favoured the Union. The Commissioner was bitterly reviled and hooted, while, in the evening of the day, several hundred persons escorted the Duke of Hamilton to his lodgings, encouraging him by loud huzzas to stand by the cause of national independence. The rabble next assailed the house of the Lord Provost, destroyed the windows, and broke open the doors, and threatened him with instant death as a favourer of the obnoxious treaty."

But the politicians in Edinburgh and London had their plans ready and were determined to pay no attention to the people. Money played an important part, and if the Lowlanders did not sell their King it cannot be denied that they sold their Parliament. The famous Flying Squadron of peers (the small Third Party who pretended to be independent) was bought, and bought cheaply.

Sir Walter Scott alleges that one of them sold his vote for eleven guineas and threw in his religion as well. Nor did the Scottish peers who accepted English bribes even show any business sense, for they allowed themselves to be bribed with their own money, and they did not notice it.

It might have been better if they had gone to a financial expert like William Paterson for advice instead of trusting themselves to the Londoners.

Those who believe that the Act of Union meant the voluntary uniting on free and equal terms of two free and equal Parliaments might study the figures of the seats allotted to the two countries in the new Parliament.

Scotland received forty-five seats in the Commons instead of the sixty-six to which its population entitled it, and in the Lords sixteen elected seats against the whole of the English peerage. Even after the modern redistribution of seats, Scotland has still a smaller representation in the Commons than is justified by her population, while her representation in the Lords is derisory. Out of more than seven hundred members there are still only sixteen elected peers of Scotland. Furthermore, those peers of Scotland who are not elected to the sixteen are ineligible for seats in the House of Commons, and are therefore the only persons over the age of twenty-one, male or female, in England and Scotland who are debarred from sitting in either House. Furthermore, whereas Oxford University has two members, and Cambridge University has two, and London University has one, and the remainder of the English Universities have two between them, the ancient and famous Universities of St Andrews, Glasgow, Aberdeen, and Edinburgh have only two members between the four. This, then, was the representation that Scotland received in exchange for the abolition of its own Parliament and the transfer of its seat of Government to the capital city of another country. It was small wonder that the common people vigorously and vehemently objected to the surrender, but the threats and the bribes from the south easily overrode the voice of the people as threats and bribes usually do.

A. V. Dicey and R. S. Rait have written:

"The removal of the Parliament of Scotland from Edinburgh produced, however, deeper evils than merely arresting the prosperity of Edinburgh. It diminished the influence of Scotsmen on legislation which might affect Scotland. The intelligence of Scotland was, in 1707, to a great extent centred in her capital city. Many of the leading men resided there. The Court of Session met there. The General Assembly of the Church met there. A leading University had its seat there. Intellectually and morally, Edinburgh represented the feeling of Scotland, or at any rate of the Lowlands, as truly as, and perhaps more truly than, during the eighteenth century, London represented the opinion of England. Edinburgh, indeed, returned but two members to the Scottish Parliament, and after the Union returned but one member to the British Parliament, and both before and after the Union the electorate of Edinburgh was ridiculously small. But, for all that, the opinion of the most important city in Scotland was certain, to tell upon the votes of the members of a Parliament whether Lords, county members, or burgh members, which met in Edinburgh. The opinion of Scotland, in short, was, before the Union, concentrated at Edinburgh, and was guided a good deal by the sentiment of the capital."

But resentment against the English could not last so long in the Lowlands as in old time. Darien was soon forgotten, as trade began to revive, and as the desire for material prosperity grew stronger and stronger. Glencoe helped to raise two Jacobite armies. Darien did not raise more than a few riots. And by the time the Highlanders began their last military adventure, in 1745, the Lowlands had made up their minds which side was going to win. Under the leadership of such men as Forbes of Culloden and, of course, the Chief of the Clan Campbell, they came down on the side of the German King. But the outlook of the country had changed to such an extent in the previous sixty years that the Lowlands did not bring their ancient violence into the war. Instead of hurling themselves into battle with their old bravery, recklessness, and stupidity, they sided with the German King only to the extent of sitting on the fence. They would neither join the Highland adventurers nor would they raise the country against them when they marched to Edinburgh and afterwards to Derby. The genius of the Lowlands was strongly turning to the new arts of commerce, which they were learning from the English as enthusiastically as in the old days they had learnt the arts of war. And so the Highlander reaped in the end what he had sowed. He had turned his back for so long upon the struggle for independence on the Border that the spirit of Bannockburn, where the two Celtic races fought side by side, had long died out, and south of the Highland Line there was less sympathy for the half-savage, Gaelic-speaking, Catholic soldiers than for the cultured, peaceful and, above all, wealthy, English with their German kings, generals, and troops. The two motives which animated the clans to fight for Prince Charles Edward were the instinctive feeling that he was the rightful King, and their loyalty to their Chiefs. But the Burgesses of the south cared very little for rightful or wrongful kings, or for clan loyalty, so long as they were allowed to continue their peaceful professions in peace, and it was obvious that their best chance of being allowed to do this lay in the triumph of Anglo-German dullness and solidity, rather than in the wildness and romance of Jacobitism. The cleavage between the two cousinly races of Scotland was never more clearly shown than in the first half of the eighteenth century. For whereas the Highlands after their defeat faded gradually, gracefully, but inevitably, into defeatism, the Lowlander had not given up one iota of his strongly individualistic character after his defeat in the political sphere, almost as crushing as Culloden in the military, in the battle of the Union in 1707.

He had lost voluntarily his militarism and his militant theology, and then, compulsorily, his politics. Not in the least daunted, he threw himself with all his vehemence into the new idea of trade.

CHAPTER XI

The Scottish Trader Abroad

Just as I digressed from my chronological sequence to say a word about the military connection of Scotland and England after the formation of the Royal Scots, so now I must digress for a moment to give an illustration of the supreme difficulty which faced, in the eighteenth and nineteenth centuries, the Scottish trader abroad. It is the same supreme difficulty which faced him at Darien and faces him today. I must deal with it at some length, for it is almost as important to my story as the date of Edward Plantagenet itself.

The illustration of this difficulty which I am going to give is the story of two Canadian trading companies. When two roving Frenchmen, Groseillier and Radisson, came to England in the 1660's with a project for trading in furs with the natives of Hudson's Bay, they were lucky enough to find one of Britain's four intelligent Highland kings on the throne. But, although it was the Highland Charles the Second who granted the Charter to the new Company, it is significant that the name of the new Company was the "Governor and Company of Adventurers of England trading into Hudson's Bay." There was no mention of Scotland when it came to business, and although the first Governor of the Company was Rupert of the Rhine, half Stuart, and the second was the Duke of York (afterwards James the Second), wholly Stuart, the Governorship very soon fell into the hands of the southerner, and the third on the list is John Churchill, the great Duke of Marlborough.

From the year 1685, in which James, Duke of York, ceased to be Governor of the Company, there is not a single Scottish name among the Governors (although the Donald Smith who afterwards became Lord Strathcona was, of course, a Scotsman), until the year 1931, when the present Governor, Mr Patrick Ashley Cooper of Aberdeen, was appointed. It was in fact, and in name, an English Company of English traders.

It took the Hudson's Bay Company nearly a hundred years to be quit of French competition in the fur trade in Canada, and when Wolfe's victory on the Plains of Abraham cleared the way for an English monopoly the prospects of the Company were good. But within the next twenty years they had to face a competition which was incomparably more ruthless and more bitter than anything which the French had put up. The North-West Company of Montreal was almost entirely composed of Highlanders banded together for trading as no body of Scotsmen had banded themselves together since Darien, and just as those who ventured in the Darien scheme found the English across their path, so the North-West Company found the Hudson's Bay. But conditions in early Canada were more suited to Highland methods than conditions in Threadneedle Street had been for Lowland. The men of the Montreal Company were sons of Wolfe's soldiers or men of the United Empire Loyalists or were fugitives from the 'Forty-five. They were accustomed to hardship and endurance, and they were prepared to use violence on the slightest provocation.

The most famous of them was Alexander Mackenzie, of Stornoway, who discovered the Mackenzie River, the greatest of all Canadian rivers. While the English Company was concentrating around Hudson's Bay itself and its immediate hinterland, the Highlanders pushed west and north-west for thousands of miles, and it is to their heroism and power of endurance and vision, to which must in justice be added their ruthlessness and unscrupulousness, that modern Canada owes its existence as a Dominion of the British Commonwealth.

The bitter competition between the two Companies could not last, for there were sufficient brains on both sides to understand that there was enough trade, enough furs, enough land for all, and in 1821 the Englishmen and Scotsmen pooled their resources and created a monopoly.

Of the Chief Factors who signed the deed poll of agreement: on the side of the Hudson's Bay Company there are five English names and five Scottish; on the side of the North-West Company there are eight Highland names, six Lowland, and one Smith, who might be anything. Of the Chief Traders who signed the deed poll: on the side of the Hudson's Bay Company there are six English names and five Highland; on the side of the North-West Company there are ten Highland names, four Lowland, one French, one English, and one Irish. From this time the new Amalgamated Company had a complete monopoly and was able to lay claim to almost the whole of the lands of Western and North-western Canada.

The story runs precisely true to the pattern which this book is tracing. The time of the amalgamation was the critical point in the history of both the North-West Company and the Hudson's Bay, and the hour of crisis found the right man ready to take control. George Simpson was born an illegitimate child at Loch Broom in Ross-shire, and after serving as a clerk in the London office of a Scottish merchant firm he went to Canada and, at the age of thirty-four, had become Governor of the Company in Canada. Simpson was the greatest of all fur traders and for nearly forty years he controlled the entire trade from Hudson's Bay to the Pacific Ocean. That might be claimed as another triumph for the ubiquitous and conquering Scot, but not all the administrative brilliance and all the trading achievements and all the continent-wide fame of George Simpson could alter the fact that in 1863 the entire Hudson's Bay Company with all its men and its assets, and its territorial claims, and its organisation which Simpson perfected, was bought lock, stock and barrel by a group of London bankers, with names such as Baring, Watkins, Head, Lampson, Meinertzhagen, Hodgson, Schroeder, and Potter. There are not many Scottish names among these.

So the story of Highland-Canadian enterprise ends in Threadneedle Street. All the work, all the heroism, all the endurance, all the energy, of the Highlanders who went from Scotland to Montreal and from Montreal out into the wilds, came back in the end to a boardroom in the City of London. It need not be added that the group of bankers did not rest content with the possession of Prince Rupert's Company. They used it with the greatest possible skill as an instrument with which to hold up the newly-born Government of Canada in order to obtain concessions for railways and telegraphs.

The moral of the tale, in case there is anyone who needs to have it pointed out, is that the supreme difficulty which has faced, and is facing, all Scots traders is this: that the road of high endeavour, endurance, far-sightedness, vision, courage, and exile, in whatever continent it is mapped out, through whatever jungle it is cut, across whatever desert it is traced, over what mountains it is laboriously scaled, is apt to lead in the end to London.

CHAPTER XII

The Industrial Revolution

Whereas all the heroism of the Scottish soldiers in the ranks of England during the years between 1689 and 1759 was only marking the end of an old song, the end of Scottish military history, the story of the Hudson's Bay Company was typical of the beginning of a new one. The military amalgamation of the fighting men of the two countries was little more than an affair of sentiment mingled with political expediency. But the commercial amalgamation was an affair of business and therefore a good deal more important.

The new song, or perhaps dirge, which was being prepared for Scotland towards the end of the eighteenth century, was being prepared, like Edward's Hammer and Knox's sermons, in the south.

The Industrial Revolution was at hand. It came sweeping northwards through the coal and iron districts, through the cotton factories of Lancashire, through Staffordshire and Yorkshire. It is, of course, impossible to lay all the blame on the English. The Industrial Revolution was exactly what the Lowlander had been looking for. It exactly suited his temperament. The long legacy of violence and ugliness which he had inherited found an outlet as perfect as the military and political and religious outlets of the past. The Manchester doctrine of *laissez faire* was in perfect accord with the unyielding individualism of the Lowland character.

And, after all, although the actual revolution, in all its beastliness and monstrosity, came from the south, it cannot, in all decency, be denied that the Lowlands played a part in its birth. It was Adam Smith who wrote the doctrine of *laissez faire* into literary and philosophic form, and it was James Watt who made the fatal experiments with the kettle and the tea-spoon which began the whole disastrous business. So, what with his temperament and his thinkers it is not altogether surprising that the Lowlander should have thrown himself with gusto into the new era of economic and mechanical novelties. Adam Smith's writing, and Watt's tea-spoon, both made a natural appeal to a race of educated and enquiring individualists, and the subsequent beastliness could

106

not, of course, in the least repel men who had heard of the English wars and still knew the Genevese religion. But the essential point is that though Adam Smith and Watt were concerned in the birth of the industrial revolution, the actual overgrown, dirty, repulsive infant came from England.

The Lowlands made the infant uglier. That was only to be expected. They made it dirtier. They made it more repulsive. The men of Lancashire and Yorkshire and Durham had been brought up in a hard school, but even so they are softer, a little, than the men of Lanarkshire and Renfrew. And Lancashire and Yorkshire and Durham did not have to receive as guests the Irish invasion to anything like the same extent. England missed a great deal which Scotland gained in that earlier Irish invasion, when Columba came with his cross to Iona. But England also missed a great deal when the Irish poor flocked into the new industrial Glasgow. So not even Wigan and Warrington are quite so awful as the strings of little mining villages between Lanark and Stirling, grey, bleak, dingy, unhappy villages. Not even Sheffield and Bradford are quite as bad as the worst parts of Glasgow.

It is the natural function of the passionate individualist to create the worst as well as the best. If he failed to create either, he would cease to become an individualist and would deserve the most disciplined regimentation. So, as the Lowlander evolved the most perfect type of industrialised slum, so he also evolved the most perfect type of industrialised man. Both, of course, are dirty, but the essential difference between them is that whereas the former is called industrialised and is inhabited by the poor, the latter is called an Industrialist and is worshipped by the rich. The Lowland's type of the former is the poorer part of Glasgow; of the latter it is Andrew Carnegie. Both were the product, or epitome, of a deadly ruthlessness. The men who herded their wageslaves into those slums cared as little for the sanctity of human life as Carnegie cared for the strikers in the great Homestead strike in 1892, but both were ruthlessly efficient in the care of machines. To care for a machine was common sense, for a machine costs money to buy and money to replace. But a man costs nothing, and a woman less, and a child least of all.

Carnegie was to the industrial revolution (he operated only in Pittsburg, but he was the apotheosis of it all) what Knox had been to the Reformation. England, introducing both movements in Britain, never approached anything quite so dreadful as either man.

It is no coincidence that Knox should have defaced the soul and the architectural beauties of Scotland to the greater glory of his God, and that Carnegie should have tried to buy salvation by defacing Scotland's soul and land with free libraries. Neither Geneva nor Pittsburg seem to me to be as beautiful as Iona.

* * *

The Lowlander of the nineteenth century took an instinctive liking to machines. The liking quickly grew into a passion, and out of this passion came a logical and important development.

For hundreds of years the English had been the supreme masters of the art of sailing ships. The outcome of that mastery was the inevitable empire which, throughout the history of Europe, those who held the sea have ultimately held on the land. The Phoenicians, Athens, Carthage, Rome, Venice, Spain, Holland, and now England, have based their land empire upon sea-power.

In the making of this maritime English empire the Scots, as a nation, or as a country of two races, played only a small part. The habit of the Border wars had distracted them from seafaring and, except for the in-shore fishermen and a few notable sea-captains, the Scots cut a poor figure afloat during the era of sail. There was no tradition of seamanship, no ever-expanding foreign commerce to protect, and very few oak trees growing in the land.

The coming of steel and steam and machines changed all that. Skill in handling a sailing-ship in a high gale is born only of instinctive experience and centuries of seafaring ancestors, and a natural sense of poetry. Skill in handling a steam-driven iron ship can be acquired by the assiduous study of books.

And the Lowlander has for a long time been a passionate believer in the value of book-learning. Midnight-oil is to him a capital substitute for many talents. When sail vanished from the seas and steam took its place English and Scottish mariners started level, from scratch as it were.

Naturally, therefore, the laborious student not only held his own with the more carefree Englishman, but passed ahead of him in the maritime ranks of the Empire, so that Scottish captains, mates, and engineers have become famous all over the world, far out of proportion to the respective populations of the two countries.

It is obvious that from the beginning of the machine-age the Lowland genius was bound to run to shipbuilding. The instinctive liking for machines, and the instinctive skill in the making of them and tending of them, was naturally focused upon Clydeside, a magnificent waterway which was also near iron and coal. It followed, therefore, that this new engineering skill should run to marine engineering. Hence came the great tradition, great in the real sense of greatness and not in the hackneyed phrase which implies that a tradition must be great simply because it is long, of Clydeside ship-building, marine-engineering, and, their corollary, mercantile marine.

The conquest of the violent seas was at last within reach of this strong and violent race. During the era of sail it had eluded them. To master the seas in a sailing-ship requires a race of poets who are also men. The Lowlander could never have produced a Drake. The Lowlander could never have produced the idea, the essential idea, which made the existence of Drake possible and thus made the existence of England possible. The wooden walls of old Scotland was an idea that could never have been understood, and the wooden walls were, therefore, never created. Because, of course, the idea is everything and the actual carrying-out of the idea is a mere matter of "the little woman round the corner" with a sewing-machine. Hawkins was the genius who created the *Revenge* and so made the destruction of the Armada possible. But Hawkins was really nothing more than the little man round the corner. He would never have been asked to make the *Revenge* if the idea of a free England, based on the sea, and born at Sluys and Les-Espagnols-sur-Mer, had not existed for three hundred years. He was a genius at his craft. But his craft only existed because of the native genius of England. In Scotland there have been many men as great as Hawkins or greater, but in Scotland there had never been the conditions in which the ship-building genius of Hawkins flowered in the era of sail.

But when the age of machines came, all changed. The steel walls of New Scotland was an idea which every craftsman could understand. He could do more than understand it. He could realise that he was helping, by his strong, individualistic skill, to create those steel walls. Each one of them was himself a Hawkins, making a new world of ships even more surely than Hawkins. For the Elizabethan was only superseding the galleon with a new, long, heavy-artillery sailing-ship. The Glasgow fitter was superseding the Argo itself.

* * *

The most perfect example of the Lowland attitude towards the industrial revolution, with the whole contrast which it implies with the defeatist Highland attitude, is to be found, of course, in the writings of an Englishman. Whenever you want a flash of poetical insight, or a piece of particularly subtle financial chicanery, or a piece of far-sighted imperialism, you are pretty safe to go to England for the ultimate example.

Rudyard Kipling wrote a poem about a Glasgow engineer. Kipling had many Lowland qualities: he loved violence and brutality, and individualism, and straightforward speech, and narrow-mindedness and success. And he worshipped machines. His poem contains all these.

The engineer in the poem, a man called Macandrew, delivers a monologue about his engine and his God, interwoven together. The language, in that oddly printed English, which is supposed by some authors to be Scots dialect, is a jumble of technical jargon and stern Calvinism. That in itself is a stroke of genius. Only a man who is inflexibly determined to make the best of things, physical and spiritual, can see his God in a crank-shaft, and the Lowlander is that man.

So Macandrew can say, in this odd printing:

> "From coupler-flange to spindle-guide I see Thy Hand,
>   O God —
> Predestination in the stride o' yon connectin'-rod.
> John Calvin might ha' forged the same — enorrmous,
>   certain, slow —
> Ay, wrought it in the furnace-flame — *my* 'Institutio.'"

There is the whole spirit of the nineteenth-century awakening on the Clyde-machines, Calvin, an engineer, and an Englishman.

But there is still one detail to be noticed in the beautiful illustration of what I have been trying to explain about the Lowland character, and its passion for vehement and hard things like connecting-rods and Calvin. That detail is, as I have also been trying to explain in a much earlier part of this book, the Englishman's romantic passion for the Highlands. Kipling, writing a long philosophical poem about a Clydeside engineer, and striking off his character to a hair's breadth, got carried away by the Highland glamour and called his hero Macandrew. There may be lots of Calvinistic engineers in Glasgow called Macandrew, but if you are writing a poem about a typical one, you ought not to allow yourself to be carried away by the glamour of another country. It would be as if you wrote an epic of the Worcestershire countryside in which the rustic hero was called Magersfontein. There may be a rustic hero in Worcestershire called Magersfontein for all I know. But the point I am making is that, if there is, he is not typical of that county. And Macandrew is not typical of the sort of man in the poem.

No Highlander of the north-west would have talked like the Macandrew of the poem, or would have accepted either Geneva or ball-bearings as essential parts of the romance of the world.

But the moment you agree that the Macandrew of the poem is a typical Lowlander and that his name ought to have been Jock Thompson, fascinated by the power of the machine and by its dividend-earning capacity, everything falls neatly into character. The machine is strong and it gives service for service.

"Interdependence absolute, foreseen, ordained, decreed,
To work, Ye'll note, at any tilt an' every rate o' speed."

Up to a point, the philosophy was the philosophy of the Stoic. Dr Gilbert Murray has written of the Stoic idea of Evolution, which was called Phusis or "the way things grow."

"Phusis shapes the acorn to grow into the perfect oak, the blind puppy in the good hound; it makes the deer to grow in swiftness to perform the function of a deer, and man to grow in power and wisdom to perform the function of a man. If a man is an artist it is his function to produce beauty; if he is a governor, it is his function to produce a flourishing and virtuous city."

To Kipling and the Lowlander it was the function of the machine to make things, whether tin-tacks or battleships, that should be as near perfection in form as the machine could make them.

So far the Lowlander and the Stoic go side by side, but Dr Murray goes on:

"True, the things that he produces are but shadows and in themselves utterly valueless; it matters not one straw whether the deer goes at ten miles an hour or twenty, whether the population of a city die this year of famine and sickness or twenty years hence of old age."

This would not suit Kipling or the Lowlander. The machine must not only be a thing of beauty, but it must pay, and its products must be sold in the markets of the world for the betterment of its owner. There must be no nonsense about producing things that are utterly valueless. That will not do at all. The machine must work beautifully and profitably.

This double function constitutes the romance of the industrial age to those Scotsmen of the south who were fortunate enough, hard-working enough, or lucky enough to succeed. But to the Highlander, in spite of what Mr Moray McLaren says, I swear it was no romance.

* * *

As the nineteenth century went on, and the passion for money-making grew and grew with each new invention and process, and with the opening of the great new markets overseas, a rich middle-class sprang up all over the south and midlands of the country. This middle-class came, of course, from the true

111

stock, hard and violent and hitherto unconquerable, and, as the true Lowland stock had always done, it inherited the paradoxical capacity to preserve its individualism and at the same time absorb new ideas and compromise with them. The building of the railways had brought Lanark very near to London, but the sturdy new middle-class was not at this time afraid of London, for all its banks, and clearing-houses, and insurance companies, and stock-brokers. He was ready to accept the new ideas which London might offer him, but he was going to use them in his own way. On this principle of combined self-reliance and self-adaptation, the new rich became richer and richer.

But his wealth, and the modern proximity of London, brought other ideas as well as those of commerce and finance. If the railways brought Lanark near to Throgmorton Street, they also brought it near to Mayfair and Piccadilly, and new social standards began to come northwards. These standards were softer and more sentimentalised than anything which the rich Lowlander, sprung from humble and stern and self-disciplined forebears, had ever known before. The English have always had more leisure in which to be soft and sentimental between their battles and their business-deals, and their long centuries of success have given them a greater inclination to sleekness. But it was all new to the Lowland middle-classes, and a certain side of his character revelled in the southern standards of life. He discovered that he could meet the famous Londoners upon grouse-moors and beside salmon-rivers, and, although at this time they were comparatively rare, even in deer-forests. He, too, could buy estates that had belonged to some unpractical, dreaming Gael and despatch the tenantry to Alberta and British Columbia. He could even buy a kilt and become romantically-minded. Charles Edward was dead long since, so by a happy idea it was unanimously resolved to resuscitate him and christen him "Bonnie Prince Charlie." With a great whoop, the echoes of which still reverberate round the world, and a great gusto, and an almost unbelievable vulgarianism, the nineteenth century threw itself upon the story of the defeated Highlanders.

Mr Moray McLaren has written the last word about the rising of 1745 and what it has become:

> "It is quite impossible, if one is at all sensitive, to say anything of what one really feels about that business. The whole thing has been so despoiled, slopped over, mucked about, by halfpenny romanticists, that no one, short of a Shakespeare, could nowadays lift it out of the morass into which it has been dragged. Its song tunes have become music-hall favourites, its stories and its traditions have become the lucrative property of any footling sentimentalist who wants to make money out of the Woolworth public. And the descendants of those who made the thing itself are mostly in America or Canada."

Anyone of whatever name, whether Blenkinsop or Jones or Guffin, whether he could claim a maternal grandmother as a member of an obscure sept of one of the clans, or whether he could not, hastened to buy a kilt and to wear it whenever possible and to boast of his long line of fighting ancestors.

The reason was partly that the glamour of the tartan had caught them, as it had caught others more illustrious than themselves. The self-made careerist who listened to the Highlander's soft web of Sales-Talk was only following the example of the First Lady of the Land. Her Majesty Queen Victoria was the great-great-great-granddaughter of that George, Elector of Hanover, who afterwards became the First George of England. He in his turn was the maternal grandson of Frederick the Fifth, the Elector Palatine who married Elizabeth Stuart, daughter of James the Sixth and First. The female side of Queen Victoria's descent came through Saxe-Coburg-Gotha, Mecklenburg-Strelitz, Saxe-Gotha, Brandenburg-Ansbach, Brunswick-Luneberg (Calle), and the Palatine. Yet Balmoral Castle was decorated freely with the Royal Stuart tartan on the strength of this connection with the Stuarts, and if the Queen, why not her loyal subjects?

But, I think, there was another deeper reason than the Highland legend for this desire of the Cymric to draw closer to the Gael. It is, when you look at it more carefully, a strange phenomenon. There are two cousins, and one is a failure, the other is a success. The cousin who is a failure has no wish to be associated with his go-ahead, pushing relation. The cousin who is a success, and who is immensely proud of his success, is desperately anxious not merely to be accepted as the cousin of the failure, but to be actually taken for his brother. Why was it?

Why did the soldiers of the Lowlands so enthusiastically identify themselves with the regiments of the north in the World War? Why did they discard their own glorious tradition of courage which had come down from the years when they, and they alone, fought for the independence of Scotland against the English? Why did they leap so eagerly into kilts and toast each other with "Slainte," the only Gaelic word they knew? Why did they look down their noses so distantly at the 52nd Lowland Division?

The roots of the answer are to be found in the growing divergence of the actual mode of life of the two cousins. During the seventeenth and eighteenth centuries the cleavage between them had been religious and political. In the nineteenth, to this cleavage was added a social one. The gap widened fast. On one side there was a remnant, living among the loveliest of scenery upon the shores of the ocean or upon the slopes of the mountains, thinking only of the past; on the other there was a quickly growing mass of population, struggling madly for a share of the new wealth, living in a filth and squalor that was undreamt of in the Middle Ages, and toiling interminable hours in dark factories and darker mines. The struggle for a bare existence was hard in the north, but at least it was a struggle in the open air, with at least a pretence of freedom around it. In the industrial belt it was a sordid and degrading slavery. Even those who fought their way out of the common degradation and managed to rise over the bodies of their contemporaries to the position of slave-driver in one of the new industries, or dividend-drawer from one of the new companies, were themselves caught in a net from which there was no escape. The new middle-classes were the slaves of respectability, of the Calvinistic Sabbath, of genteel gloom, of solid granite houses, of aspirations to town-councillorships, of money, of conventional marriages, of endless child-bearing, and of bigoted ministers.

High in the heavens above these material and psychological slaves there was a wonderful land of freedom and romance and chivalry. From the prison of a fourteen-hour day, or of a mass of repressions and inhibitions, they looked out upon a paradise of heather and hills, where the men wore eagles' feathers and diamond brooches, where the women were tall and graceful and fearless, where silver-hilted rapiers slithered against each other in the moonlight upon the sands of the ocean, where sloe-eyed ladies saved the lives of handsome and unfortunate princes, and where sea-fairies danced in lace coats and embroidered gowns to the pipe-music of ghostly M'Crimmons. They lifted up their eyes from the pit-shafts and the chimney-smoke unto the hills, and they saw the red deer upon the mountain-sides and the white hares among the birch-woods and upon the moors, and they saw the rollers of the Atlantic among the Isles, and they heard the little waters of Shira and Aora, and they felt the smells of the herring in Strathlachlan and of the salt seas and of the peat-smoke, and of the juniper and bog-myrtle. All that they heard and saw and dreamt. They did not see the survivors of the clans as they huddled in overcrowded bothies, and toiled endlessly upon patches of land that were too sterile for sheep, and went to the fishing in leaky boats, and gathered seaweed on the landowner's beaches. That side of the Highland panorama did not appear in the mirage. To the pent-up industrialist, all the mirage was lovely and romantic. He thought that every tiny part of the life of the Highlander, past, present, and future, was the exact antithesis of his own sordid and smoky lot and was therefore infinitely desirable. It represented for him all the romance which he would never know in his own existence, all the wildly glamorous eccentricities of an aristocratic chivalry which he would never meet, all the high political dreams which would never disturb his hard head as he sat, late at night, in his counting-house and reckoned up the month's turnover and compared it with the turnover of the corresponding month of the previous year. For he too was a Celt. He was blood brother to the Welshman who, if he has created the horrors of Ebbw Vale and Rhondda and Swansea, has also sung at Eistedfodds and preached revivalism and dreamt dreams. The Lowlander's place might be in the counting-house, but somewhere in his far distant heredity there was a time when he, too, was free on a mountain-side and made his fires of pinewood and peat instead of broken coke. The untraceable twistings of the Celtic heredity had turned him to hard commercial realism, just as it had turned the Welshman, but it had left a little memory of earlier times when realism was not everything. So he gazed from his neat, lace-curtained, stone-built house, or from his hideous abomination in the slums of Glasgow, across the Highland Line and tried to live again the story of Charles Edward and Flora MacDonald and to pretend that there, but for the Grace of God and the teachings of John Calvin, went Jock and Maggie Smith.

But the newly rich middle-classes who were thus softening, becoming sentimental and following eagerly after a will-o'-the-wisp glamour of the Gael, knew perfectly well that this change was coming over their characters and they bitterly resented it. They liked luxury, but they hated the idea that anyone should accuse them of being luxurious. They began to admit the existence of sentiment, but ashamedly, as if it was some monstrous vice. And so these stern individualists, descendants of the barons who had held the Marches against the English, became outwardly tougher than ever in order to conceal their shameful weakness. They worked harder than ever. They bullied the poor, and they set out to make a world-wide reputation for themselves as ruthless and successful careerists. Only by succeeding in the material world would they be able to conceal the change. The more Anglicised they became, the more patriotic in their praise of Scotland and the more vigorously anti-English did they appear to be.

The spirit of the Cameronians was revived. The Sabbath day was observed with a ghastly rigidity and intolerance that has become a by-word. The countryside was cruelly desecrated to make way for factories. A system of licensing laws was enforced that made the Scottish public-house the horrible den which it is today, and utterly destroyed the spirit of good-comradeship and quiet geniality which still lives in the English country inn, and as a substitute for which in Scotland a bogus legend of conviviality has had to be invented under a bogus legend of Robert Burns. And, side by side with this exorcism of Bacchus was a stern and fantastically hypocritical attempt to exorcise Venus as well. Love-making was as villainous a sin as gaiety, but the sweating of children in mines and the flogging of children in homes were true signs of grace.

* * *

The gentry made no attempt to conceal the direction in which their sympathies lay. They became almost completely Anglicised, and followed, in fact, in the second half of the nineteenth century the footsteps of the courtiers who came to London with James the Sixth and First in 1603, and of the nobility who went to London in 1707, after the Union of the Parliaments. It became fashionable in the eyes of many of the gentry to speak with a pure English accent, and it has always been a source of distress and a cause of annoyance to them that the Highlander finds it so much easier to go straight from Gaelic or, at any rate, from Gaelic fathers and grandfathers, to a pure English accent, than the Lowlander who has behind him centuries of uncouth variation of the English tongue. It also became fashionable to send sons to English public schools, and when, at about this time, the Scottish gentry founded the Scottish public schools for their sons, they chose as their model, not the ancient Scottish Grammar Schools, but Winchester, and Eton, and Harrow.

But though the gentry followed the old nobility into England, so to speak, the new wealthy middle-class, however much it might be softening, remained essentially Scottish. It could not, indeed, do otherwise. Its roots were too deep, and its new position in the world too recent, to admit of a sudden change. But it was always on the look-out for change. There has never been anything static about the Lowlander, with his restlessly enquiring mind, his contempt for tradition, and his refusal to accept the opinions and recommendations and comminations of others. He is "for ever curiously testing new opinions and courting new impressions, never acquiescing in a facile orthodoxy." So he moves steadily on his ever-changing road, from war to religion, from religion to commerce, and from, or rather with, commerce to politics.

CHAPTER XIII

Victorian Liberalism

To generalise about the beginnings and origins of any great movement of ideas is always foolish. But if we can accept as a general theory that nineteenth-century Liberalism was generated by the French philosophers of the eighteenth century, together with Adam Smith's economic ideas, together with the essential key-stone of the arch, namely, the sweeping away of the idea of Privilege and its replacement by the theory of Equality before the Law, the key-stone which was forced into position by the victories of Napoleon, if we can accept that as a general theory, then we go far towards understanding the enthusiastic acceptance by middle-class Scotland of Victorian Liberalism.

The new rich class was anxious to rise on the social ladder and also anxious to prevent a central government from interfering in their right to oppress the poor. They welcomed eagerly therefore the double teaching that privilege ought to be abolished in society and that *laissez-faire* ought to be the rule in industry. They wanted to climb from rung to rung, but they also wanted to make certain that the ladder was firmly planted upon the necks of the poor. Mr Colin Walkinshaw has, I think, accurately described the growth of Liberalism in Scotland:

"The poor and the middle-class alone remained genuinely Scottish. To each the new gospel of liberalism brought a special promise — to the poor the hope of justice and of a new power to protect themselves against oppression; to the newly enriched, the merchants and manufacturers, the professional people, an end of social inequalities, and of the moral right of governments to interfere with the proper middle-class business of money-making."

This feeling that the new creed might bring a change to the downtrodden was so strong that even the Highlands and the Islands, traditionally Tory and Jacobite, turned to Liberalism, almost more enthusiastically than the south, and today the outer fringe of the north-west still retains its beliefs.

But even in embracing this political creed so enthusiastically the Lowlander did not embrace it blindly. Indeed it is doubtful if the Lowlander ever does anything blindly. From the middle-class down to the lowest worker every Scottish Liberal expected to gain some material advantage. In other words, like everything else, Liberalism had to deliver the goods or be scrapped for something else which would. As early as 1888 the Scottish Parliamentary Labour Party was founded by Keir Hardie, Cunninghame Graham, and a handful of friends, to take the place of a creed which these men, either through far-sightedness or through impatience, felt would be of no real use to the labouring masses of Scotland. But whether it was impatience or whether it was vision that impelled them to break away, events proved that temporarily, at any rate, they were right. Liberalism had failed in the function of the machine. It had failed to repay service with service. The World War led to the almost universal destruction of Liberalism in Europe, and Keir Hardie's Party stepped into its place. The Lowlander was ready for the new movement, as he had always been for any movement. He flung himself into Socialism fanatically and when, in 1922, the British Parliamentary Labour Party reached its highest numbers up to that time, the spearhead was the violent, energetic, and individualistic group from the Clyde. The leader of the whole British Labour Party, although he was not a Clydesider, came from Lossiemouth, and the English members had to sit back and play a minor role in the new Socialist partnership. The English members continued to sit back. They knew instinctively, as the English always have known, that they had only to sit back and time will do the rest. Today, only nineteen years after the Clydesiders, with their allies from Dundee and the Lanarkshire mines, ruled the roost, the Socialist contingent of the parliamentary handful of Scottish members is divided into three parties.

That the Scottish Labour Party should be damped by the English and should split into three parts is exactly according to form. As we have seen, any Scot who comes into contact with England becomes softened and sentimentilised. That he also becomes, at the same time, bamboozled is another matter, with which I will deal later. But of his gradual softness, with its incipient romanticism, there is no doubt.

When the wild parliamentarians of 1918 and 1922 came south, they intended to pulverise the institutions of Westminster into a thinner dust than Prince Charles ever contemplated for the Hanoverian throne. But whereas the Prince turned back and was defeated, the Clydesiders stayed and were defeated. Neither Prince of 1745 nor engineer-republican of 1922 grasped the eternal truth that contact with the English means ultimate defeat unless you are Irish or, like George Washington, English yourself. The engineer-republicans stayed at Westminster and, instead of the iron entering into their souls, by a curious but completely Anglo-Saxon inversion, the iron went out of their souls. They came from the steel-yards of Clyde, and gradually they were absorbed into the cotton-wool of Westminster.

The Lowlands, like the Highlands, run true to character. The former's truth to character may be a sensitive appreciation of the grace-notes in a pibroch, while the latter's may be an equally sensitive appreciation of the ten-thousandth part of an inch to which a machine is running — both forms are poetry — but the point is that both run true in all main circumstances.

Here, at Westminster, we have a band of Lowland political adventurers, strong, violent, and individualistic men. They come, as all Scots marauders try to do, to London. They arrive. They harry the English. They ease off a little in their harrying: They gradually sink into acquiescence. They finally sink into cotton-wool. They reach, in fact, the place where the English want them to be, and have always gently intended them to be. But though they have fallen victim to the deadly assimilation, as other men have fallen victim before, they retain enough of the Lowland individualism and pugnacity to fight among themselves. The spirit of the fifteenth-century barons is still alive, where each man's hand was against every other's, but preferably against his neighbour's, and Mr Maxton of Glasgow can lead the Independent Labour Party of four, and Mr Gallacher of West Fife can lead the Communist Party of himself, into almost as much vehemence against the Socialists as against the Capitalists.

So the great nineteenth-century political enthusiasm has been wrecked between the two rocks that are always in the channel of south Scotland. The Scylla is Individualism. The Charybdis is England.

There was always a chance in the old days of reaching safety by holding close to Scylla. There are those who would voluntarily be swept for ever into the pool of Charybdis. The middle course is disaster. A tamed individualist is as meaningless as a pink Socialist, and a good many of Scotland's politicians are both.

CHAPTER XIV

The Three Great Games in Lowland Scotland

This brief summary of the history of the Lowlander in his relation to England brings us near to our own day.

But before I go on to a consideration of his character, and with that, his political and intellectual future, there is one other aspect of his life which ought to be glanced at.

I have said a little about the Highlander's games and how they have degenerated into a sort of Roman Triumph; how the lovely splendour is now exhibited for the benefit of the tourist and the visitor, how the prizes are all won by professional, peripatetic athletes, and how, in fact, the south has spoiled them.

The south has also had its effect upon the Lowlander's games.

* * *

The three great games in Lowland Scotland are, Golf, Association football, and Rugby football. The first of these is the old game of certain parts of Scotland near the sea. The second is the game of the new democracy everywhere. The third, except where the Northern Union game is played, is essentially the game of the gentry in Britain.

Taking these in order; golf provides a common meeting-ground for all classes,

> "The Lord High Coachman on the box,
> The Lord High Bishop orthodox,
> The Lord High Vagabond in the stocks,"

all play golf in those parts where golf has always been traditionally played.

The golf-links (a phrase which England has borrowed to describe any mud-heap, or acreage of dusty clay upon which the golf-ball is struck) is an expression of the Lowland belief in the natural equality of mankind. Every man is equal before the laws of golf, and there is no privilege or favour. There are, of course, a few places in Scotland which conform to the old established English principle that the poor are all very well in their way, but that in certain selected spots they should be neatly tucked away out of sight of the rich. Such places are Gleneagles and Cruden Bay. But they are rare; and, on the whole, golf in Scotland is within the financial reach of anyone who is within geographical reach of a golf-links.

The Scot, as a general rule, is intensely proud of golf. It is his chief contribution — curling being the second — to the pastimes of the world, and it is very high on the list of world-popularity. (The suggestion that it originated in Holland, though supported by the pictures of several Old Masters, is ill-received north of the Tweed.) He is never tired of repeating how, in the Middle Ages, the practice of golf sadly interfered with practice of archery, and how one of the James's ordered that it should be "utterly cryit downe," and how the Great Marquis, Montrose himself, played a round on the first day of his honeymoon, and how the courtiers of James the Sixth and First brought the game to England and founded the Royal Blackheath Club, the oldest in the world, in 1608. All this is part of the saga.

The rules for acquiring proficiency at the game were handed down from generation to generation, and when, in the middle of the nineteenth century, people began to discover that there is money to be picked up in moderate but pleasing quantities, in the writing of books about games, these rules for becoming a good golf-player were analysed, dissected, and written down. The writers of these books had, of course, to find or to invent sufficient material to make into a book. There is no money to be made by jotting down two rules of two words each and one of four words on a half-sheet of note-paper and then trying to sell it. The public simply will not be taken in by that sort of thing. Yet it was soon discovered that such was indeed the case and that the fundamental instructions contained only eight words between the three of them: Slow back: Follow through: Eye on the ball. In consequence the books of instruction had to be made up of amplification, repetition, and variation on these three themes — just as a piper builds up his pibroch or Wagner his opera — with some statistics thrown in to make weight, and accounts of famous matches, and character-sketches of prominent players, and, inevitably, the Rules of Golf *in extenso*. This last device was the most satisfactory of all as it entailed no work for the author beyond the labour of despatching a copy of the rules to the printer with a short covering letter.

On these three maxims, then, Scottish golf flourished on the coast of Ayrshire, on the coasts of the Lothians, in the fields round Edinburgh, and amid the sand-dunes of the Kingdom of Fife, and Angus, and the Mearns, and Aberdeenshire.

And then the English discovered the game. At first no harm was done, for although England quickly produced the best amateur player of the day in the son of a Cheshire hotel-keeper, he played in the traditional style of Scotland. Mr John Ball's only contribution to the game was that he played it rather better than all the amateurs and almost all the professionals of the day.

But soon after Mr Ball's appearance a real menace arose in the Channel Islands, about as far from St Andrews as it is possible to be on British soil. Harry Vardon was not merely unquestionably the greatest golf-player of the age. He was a genius who invented his own methods. He played with a new stance, a new grip, a new swing, and his successes were so phenomenal that naturally everyone tried to copy him. The old maxims were forgotten, and a new generation grew up, and a new flood of books of instruction were composed which contained just as much padding as the old ones, but, of course, omitted the three talismans of our forefathers. The older Scottish golfers remained true to the Scottish style. The younger were seduced by the Englishry.

Nemesis followed the sacrilege. Vardon, the genius, had to step down at last and his disciples, without his genius, were left to face the post-war invasion of American golfers. The result was almost ludicrous. The Americans were victorious when and how they liked, and a great wail — like the wail which arose over Athens on the night when the news of the defeat at Kynoscephalæ arrived — arose over the British golfing-world. "What is wrong with British golf?"

Fifty wrong answers were given, but the right one was there for all to see. British golf was English. That was all. American golf, taught by the hundreds of Scottish professionals who had gone to America with the old pre-Vardon teaching, was Scottish golf. The American swung his club back slowly, he kept his eye on the ball, and he had a long sweeping follow-through, and he won our championship for years and years in succession.

Then the economic pendulum swung the other way. The American golf clubs suddenly found themselves not so rich as they once had been, and the Scottish assistant-professional discovered that it was better to stay at home than to go to America in search of employment.

Furthermore, numbers of Scottish golfers, who had been established in America, came home again and brought back with them the three talismans which had been abandoned in the pursuit after Channel Island gods. And so Scottish golf went back to the principles which the Great Marquis learnt, and which those who sneaked away from the archery-butts practised, and which the courtiers brought down to Blackheath — the principles of the Slow Swing, the Head Down, and the Follow-through.

Thus, at long last, the old game is coming, via the United States, into its own again.

But the English effect upon the Scottish game has been even more powerful, and disastrous, than the mere temporary alteration of the style and swing.

They have imported into it their native atmosphere of superiority and magnificence. Quite unintentionally, without a doubt, the Oxford and Cambridge Golfing Society has, in the post-war years, exercised a sort of hypnotic influence over the young golfers of Scotland. Year after year the young players of Scotland massed themselves with desperate determination. Year after year the Southerners won. Sir Ernest Holderness, Messrs. Wethered and Tolley, and other English players were always to be relied on at the crucial point; the Scottish players were not, and so, between 1920 and 1936, no Scot living in Scotland won the Amateur Championship of the native game of his country. The only flicker of the old spirit of Bruce and Wallace has shone in the annual international golf-match against England. Here a deep and passionate resolve to defeat the enemy of centuries animates the Scots. Here for a moment the superiority complex is forgotten. Here a fiery breath of hostility sweeps over the links, and, as a rule, the English are beaten. It must be admitted, however, that it is not simply a patriotic fervour on the one side that produces this result. There is also a contributory lack of intense seriousness on the other. The Scots are fighting Bannockburn over again; the English are having a pleasant day's golf. The Scots are desperately anxious to win; the English want to play well — who does not? — and do not much care who is the winner. It need hardly be added that this attitude of bland and slightly cynical indifference maddens the Scots almost beyond endurance. There are few things more exasperating than an adversary who treats a contest which involves national honour as if it were a mere game, as, of course, it is.

Scotland has accepted many modifications of the game, and of its accessories, from England, and at least two from America. The American two are steel shafts instead of hickory, and standardised sets of numbered iron-clubs. Gone is the lovely ritual of choosing a new club in the professional's shop, the testing of the shafts, the examination of the "lie" of the head, the long discussion with the professional on the respective merits of a score of possible choices, and the proud display of the ultimate choice to the connoisseurs in the club-room. All that has vanished. Now you buy a mechanically perfected set of irons, eight or nine at a time, not the product of a craftsman, but of a factory system of mass-production, and you pay a heavy price for them. They are numbered instead of named, and, with the spread of their hateful popularity, they are steadily forcing the traditional names of the clubs out of use. They bear the same relation, in fact, to an old-fashioned club as a convict bears to an honest man.

When I was a boy, in the years before the war, the irons which a golfer carried were a cleek (or driving iron), a mid-iron, an approaching-iron, a heavy mashie, perhaps also a light mashie, a mashie-niblick (an importation from England after the successes with it of J. H. Taylor, an English professional), a niblick, and a putter. There might also be a queer club or two, peculiar to the individual, for the playing of some special shot or other, and usually called by some such name as "the curly-necked iron with the cracked shaft," or the "rusty mashie which I picked up at Musselburgh."

Nowadays a golfer carries a Number One iron, a Number Two, a Three, Four, Five, Six, Seven, Eight, and heaven knows how many more, and a putter. Each stroke is played in the identical way — as nearly as possible — as every other stroke, and the varying loft and power of the different clubs theoretically does the rest.

These are America's contributions to the game. In the matter of costume, England made short work of the delightful red coat with its brass buttons, which was once the gay uniform of the links, and introduced, instead of the old-fashioned trousers, those dreadful baggy cylinders which are called "plus-fours." With these fearful garments came gaudy stockings, and, too-often, tasselled garters and shooting brogues with fringed flaps over the instep. Scotland swallowed the new prescription wholesale, as she did later the leather jacket fastened with that odd device called the "zipper," the bright-coloured jumper tucked inside the belted "plus-fours," and the parti-coloured black and white shoes. And now, in this year of 1937 in which I am writing, England has sartorially sobered down and dresses on the golf-links and golf-course in a style not unlike that of the Scottish player of 1900, while young Scotland is still too often tricked out in the gaudy fashions of the English player of the middle nineteen-twenties.

Then there has been the simplification of golf-courses. This is based on the commercial side of the game as it is played today. Whenever golf is played within a reasonable distance of a big English city, it becomes expensive. Land is dear, overhead charges are high, subscriptions soar. Therefore the club secretary and club committee are incessantly anxious to maintain the club membership at the highest possible figure in order that the bar-takings may keep the club out of bankruptcy. The device which the English have evolved in order to achieve this end is the simplification of the golf-course. The idea is that the bad player, who is invariably described as "the backbone of the game," prefers that conditions should be as easy as possible, and that if he gets into a bunker he likes to pat the ball out of it with a putter, and that if he gets into the thickest rough on the course he likes to find a brassey-lie, and that if he gets into a divot-mark on the fairway he is entitled to ask for the return of his subscription. In accordance with this theory, the English have cut and levelled the rough, and shallowed the bunkers, and chemicalised the greens, to such an extent that there is hardly a single course in the whole of England which a first-class American golfer might not reasonably expect to hole in sixty-six or sixty-seven strokes. A perfect example of this is to be found in the beautiful old course at Sunningdale. Before the qualifying rounds of the Open Championship were played there in 1926 it was the proud boast of the Committee that the course had never been holed in a competition in less than seventy strokes. Mr R. T. Jones, of Atlanta, Georgia, holed it in sixty-six and sixty-eight, in his consecutive qualifying rounds. Chemicals had done their work, and Mr Jones did the rest.

But, although the lesson was painfully clear, Scotland as usual did not flinch. She boldly followed England's lead and began to chemicalise and simplify. And so now the distinctive feature of the great seaside links, such as St Andrews and Carnoustie and Balgownie, has been sadly diminished. Whereas in the old days the ground might become bare and hard, and the only way to get near the hole was to play the beautiful running stroke that trickled on and on, over slopes and hillocks and hollows as J. E. Laidlay used to play it, and as even now Mr Lionel Munn can play it, until at last it reached the green, now there is thick, lush, verdant, sulphate-induced grass everywhere, and the player can take his Number Sixteen iron (in happier, gentler days, a light mashie) and whack the ball a mile into the air with full confidence that, on descending, it will bite into the grass, and hardly bound more than a yard or two.

In other words, the distinction between the sandy links on which the game was born and the muddy parks in which the game is becoming standardised, is being steadily reduced, and no cheep of protest has gone up from Scottish throats. On the contrary, you will hear Scottish green-committees taking pride in the velvety softness of their turf, and boasting of the similarity of the texture of their grass with that of Sunningdale or Addington.

* * *

Scottish Rugby football owes its birth and its popularity to the same movement which established the Scottish Public Schools, the same movement which has turned the faces of the gentry towards England ever since 1603.

To play Rugger is part of the same instinct as acquiring an English accent. It is, basically, part of the road to the south. But the Scottish gentlefolk have never been able to grasp an English paradox in this business of Rugger. The game, and the Public School, are both symbols of the gentry. Association football is essentially a symbol of democracy. Therefore the Scottish schools have whole-heartedly, and logically, accepted Rugger and pay little attention to the other game. What they cannot understand is why such schools as Winchester, Harrow, Eton, Malvern, Repton, and Shrewsbury, should descend to the people's game, nor why gentlemen in England should take an interest in the affairs of the Corinthian amateur Soccer players. They themselves take very little interest in their own famous amateur team, Queen's Park, which holds its own week after week, year after year, against the best professional of the Scottish League and which produced R. S. McColl, the greatest of all Scottish players. How many Fettesian-Lorettonians have ever heard of him?

The game of Rugby football is suited to the Lowlanders' temperament for one thing only, and that is its violence. He can understand that. But all the rest is alien to him. Two details from the Scottish method of playing will show at once what I mean. For years and years the authorities in charge of the game in Scotland have refused to allow the national fifteen to play with identification numbers upon their backs. The English, Wesh, and Irish fifteens are numbered so that the spectator can distinguish between the players as they throw each other savagely to the ground. But the Scots are unnumbered. The reason which is always given for this is that Rugger is a team-game, and that the individual ought not to be, and does not desire to be, distinguished apart from his team-mates. This theory of the team-spirit is, I need hardly add, a purely English theory which has been adopted by the Scots against all their traditions of politics, war, society, games, and religion, and it is simply a piece of muddled thinking to advance the English theory of the team-spirit in defence of a practice to which the English themselves, with their unfailing sense of compromise, do not adhere.

Actually, the reason why the Scottish fifteen is not numbered must surely be quite different. Surely it is not because Rugby is a team-game, but because the Scottish authorities know perfectly well that the Scotsman will never play a team-game if he can help it. So long as the Scot is not identifiable by a large number on his back, there is no incentive for him to play in his normal individualistic style. As he is certain to be lost in the crowd anyway, whether he likes it or not, he might just as well play in the dull old English style and gain the credit for being a good party-man. But put a big number on his back, and he instantly becomes a Scot, an individual, a creature whose one aim is to shine by himself, a creature to whom his fourteen colleagues mean nothing. That, I am sure, is why the Scottish authorities will not allow their fifteens to be numbered. They know enough about the national character to understand that the players cannot be trusted to refrain from the national luxury of legitimate self-advertisement.

The second argument I would put forward to show that this is essentially an alien game is the tradition, born at Inverleith and carried on at Murrayfield, that the way to play the "handling code" (a technical expression among certain kinds of sporting-journalists) is to play it with your feet rather than with your hands. The Scottish forwards are traditionally trained to dribble the awkward, oval-shaped ball along the ground, and the Scottish crowd is traditionally trained to encourage them with cries of "Feet, Scotland, feet." This custom was obviously derived from the days when Scottish gentlemen played Association football, before the influx of Anglophilism, and it has lasted long after Mr W. W. Wakefield, the English captain of the early post-war years and incomparably the greatest of modern forwards, taught his forwards to throw the ball about from hand to hand, and not to use their feet unless it was absolutely unavoidable.

But although it is admiration of the Old School Tie which makes the north so devoted to Rugby football, it cannot be denied that the same spirit of Bannockburn animates the Calcutta Cup match against the hereditary foe as animates the Scottish golfer. Wales and Ireland and even France, perhaps especially France, may defeat Scotland. It does not matter. It is a pity, but no more. The Calcutta Cup is altogether different. Each year Flodden has to be avenged. And always against an infuriating enemy who cannot remember exactly what Flodden is.

In 1923 I went to Twickenham to see the Calcutta Cup match. Scotland had a celebrated line of three-quarter backs, a magnificent full-back, a stout set of forwards, and a sound pair of halves. We shouted ourselves hoarse in the confident expectation of seeing the much-vaunted unbroken record of Twickenham broken at last. England won by nineteen points to nil, a record score in a Calcutta Cup match. Incredulous, stunned, we dispersed in silence to our homes. Waterloo Station, the terminus of the Twickenham line, was like a morgue, The English, anxious not to hurt our feelings, crept away as if they had lost their nearest and dearest friends. Two years later, the Scottish fifteen broke the Twickenham record at last with a large score. There was pandemonium at Waterloo. Eightsome reels were danced on the platforms, foursomes in the refreshment-rooms. The skirling of bagpipes mingled with the whistles of the trains and the triumphant yells of the dancers. The English watched delightedly, just as an uncle will watch the gambols of a favourite nephew.

* * *

The democratic game of Soccer is played in every town and village in Scotland, not as a social distinction, nor as one more praiseworthy attempt to imitate the lordly southerner, but as an art. Being an incomparably more difficult game than Rugby, it provides correspondingly greater scope for the educated and for the individualist. The intelligent and the quick-thinking and the expert technicians of the Soccer field are not faced with the imminent menace of seeing all their artistry brought to nothing by a charge of heavy oafs. They are not interrupted in the middle of an intricate manoeuvre by the thick hands of a sixteen-stone lout grabbing them round the neck and hurling them to the ground. And this, in consequence, is a game that exactly suits the genius of the Scot.

Association football in England is a skilful game played at an astonishing speed. The exponents of it run swiftly hither and thither, and the cry is all for pace and more pace and still more pace. The moment a player finds himself in possession of the ball he concentrates on passing it on to a colleague at the earliest possible moment. He seldom tries to execute an advance on his own.

The result is a tendency towards standardisation. There is very little difference in skill between those who are chosen to represent England in international matches and a large number of those who are not. The team at the top of the league table may be only a small number of "points" ahead of a team which is almost at the bottom.

Things are different in Scotland. The game is slower, and there is more scope for the individual genius. Consequently individual geniuses are more frequently produced and the English clubs will pay fabulous sums in "transfer-fees" for them when they appear. So we have the odd spectacle of a country with a population of less than six millions, and very little money, and not more than six clubs in the highest rank, more than holding its own with a country of forty millions and great wealth and dozens of big professional clubs. Sheer skill, control of the ball, and the development of the native talent for educated individualism, are more than a match for the dazzling speed and team-work of the English. It is not an exaggeration to say that the two finest players in post-war English Soccer have also been among the slowest, Alex James, the Scottish captain of the famous Arsenal team, and Andy Wilson, the Scottish captain of the Chelsea team.

* * *

A certain amount of cricket is played in Scotland, but the climate is against the production of first-class home-made batsmen. The wickets, being softer and less highly doctored than English wickets, naturally favour the bowler, and high scores are uncommon.

There is one point, however, about Scottish cricketers which should be noticed. The endearing but rather unpractical spirit of the English in the matter of treating a game as a game has always put them at a considerable disadvantage in their cricket matches against the touchy citizenry of Australia. The Antipodean has a desperate Will to Win, and a passionate distaste for defeat. The Englishman has neither, and, between the years of 1920 and 1930, he only won seven Test matches — as they are called for some reason — and lost fifteen. Furthermore, the next series, that of 1932, was due to be played on the Australians' own grounds, against a tremendous phalanx of batting, headed by the master-batsman of the age.

But, for the first time in cricket history, the English went out to play their national game under the leadership of a Scot, and no ordinary Scot at that. For Mr Douglas Jardine is a descendant of a grim Border race, accustomed for a thousand years to repel and to invade the Southerner. There was no soft-hearted spirit of compromise about Mr Jardine. He was the leader, and he was resolved to lead in the grim old Border style. It is true that he nearly drove the Australian continent into open secession and almost disrupted the imperial structure. But that for him was a side-issue. He went to Australia to win, and he won.

Needless to add, the easy-going English dropped him instantly, apologised to the seething continent, and, when the Australians came to the Mother Country for the next series of Test matches, their hosts, by playing a sort of second eleven, tactfully allowed the visitors to win.

CHAPTER XV

The English Influence

I think it may be detected by this time by the alert and the quick-witted that what I am trying to prove is that the key to the story of Scotland, both the Gaelic and the Cymric parts, is England. The English influence has been the dominating influence. Whenever its tide was on the ebb, Scotland's task was to build dykes against its return. When its tide was at the flood, it was Scotland's problem to drive back the waters and set to work laboriously again to reclaim the land and prepare against another flood.

As we have seen, the Highlander's part in the struggle was negligible. He crumbled at a touch. The struggle has been between Lowlander and Englishman

In his dealing with the Lowlander the English genius has perfectly flowered. In the beginning he tried brutal bludgeoning, which had succeeded him so well in Wales and was to succeed him for so long in France. But in Scotland he found himself against a man who was as tough as himself in the field, and was imaginative enough to make up in patriotism what he lacked in generalship and archery. The Englishman, incredulous at this unexpected resistance, went on battering for a great many years, and it was not until two hundred and fifty years had elapsed that he admitted he was wrong and tried a new method.

This is one of the most dangerous and bewildering traits of the Englishman, that he may suddenly, even if it takes two hundred and fifty years to reach to that point of suddenness, admit himself wrong. It might be thought to be an engaging characteristic, a kindly, gentlemanly characteristic. In reality, it is very dangerous, because it is invariably the prelude to a new line of attack, and an adversary who has been successful in resisting frontal attacks for a long time is apt to become careless about his flanks.

However, the second Anglo-Saxon invasion, the Reformation, was not more successful than the first, and the religious turmoils left Scotland still independent.

Again the English changed their line, and this time they tried flattery. If only Edinburgh's nobility and Edinburgh's culture and Edinburgh's statesmen could be lured to London, the backbone of Scotland would be broken. These new tactics were the exact opposite of the Grecian wooden horse at Troy. The English built a great wooden horse, called the Union of the Parliaments, and dumped it down outside the Parliament House in Edinburgh. Sir Robert Walpole whistled, "Dilly, Dilly, come and be killed," until the Scottish Parliament had all safely clambered inside the horse. Then the English tied stout ropes on to it and tugged it triumphantly down the London road and deposited it within a few yards, within a stone's throw as you might say, of the Stone of Destiny. It was their second great capture.

The next move was to make their prisoners contented. At first this was not so easy, as there was the unfortunate affair at Darien to be lived down. But the Jacobite risings were a great help in inducing a quiet oblivion over the financial past. It was true that the City of London had directly or indirectly suppressed the Darien Company and had thereby caused great distress in Scotland. But it was equally true that a Jacobite success in 1715 or 1745 might have directly or indirectly suppressed the City of London itself, and that would not at all have suited the stout burghers of the Lothians or of the south-west, who were beginning to grasp the fact that a financial and commercial connection with Lombard Street was going to be a great deal more profitable in the future than ever a sentimental connection with Versailles and St Germain had been in the past. And profits seemed to those stout burghers to be growing more and more important than sentiment. They did not understand their own souls. They did not realise to what extent they were going to be swayed by sentiment later on, at the expense of their profits.

But in the meantime, the material advantages of the Union of the Parliaments became more obvious in every decade, as the machine-age began and grew, and so the spiritual and intellectual disadvantages were hastily pushed into the background and ignored. Whereas the Bruce and Black Douglas had said: "Let us save our souls, even if it means rejecting every material advantage which England can bring us," in the eighteenth century their descendants were beginning to say: "Let us accept every material advantage which England can bring us, and let the salvation of our souls go hang."

They were not all saying it, for in the eighteenth century there was a vigorous budding of a native intellectual vigour which had been stifled by the military and theological violence for so long, but there was a distinct tendency to begin to say it. Voltaire had written: "It is from Scotland that we receive rules of taste in all the arts, from the epic poem to gardening," but certain people, especially in the south, were inclined to suggest that neither from the composition of epic poems nor from the practice of horticulture was any considerable financial return likely. This attitude grew stronger and more resolute as the material advantages of the industrial era grew increasingly more apparent. That the seeds of a Scots revival of creative literature were being sown in the eighteenth century is made very clear by Mr William Power in his *Literature and Oatmeal*. He describes how the Remnant of the Kirk "had a vision of a real Christian State, in which social justice should reign," and how their influence and the "tolerant philosophy of Francis Hutcheson" helped to re-create the intellectual development of Scotland which reached its highest point during the eighteenth century in Hume and Adam Smith.

But the eyes of the Lowlands were strained more and more intensely away from the new native culture to the new machines, and in the nineteenth century there was no intellectual harvest from the seeds which had been sown in the eighteenth. The new beginnings of this crop were trampled down by the heavy feet of men who were building factories or were stifled by the fumes from the chimneys. And so once again the hand of England fell across the country. After the death of Walter Scott — and he was never a Scottish writer in the sense of being part of a native revival — the cash value of epic poetry and gardening was seen to be non-existent, and the whole country turned away from such contemptible pursuits to the manlier task of making money. The country might be in chains, but, some at least of the chains were made of gold. And the fortunate few who were making money were delighted in their golden chains. Those who were not making money, but were simply toiling in slums, were not consulted about the measure of delight which their iron chains afforded them. But all were prisoners.

The next move in the game was a subtle one, so subtle indeed that it would have been written down as subconscious if it was not so perfectly in harmony with the English genius. The tough and stubborn Cymric Celt had been defeated and caught at last, and was being compelled to enjoy his defeat by a new material prosperity. But that was not enough. At any moment the blood of the Douglases or of the Cameronians might reassert itself — after all, it had its roots in those centuries when it defied even the Romans, whereas the industrial revolution was only a few decades old — and the struggle might begin again. Something more than a golden chain was necessary. There was even the possibility that the gold might give out.

So the English poetical, imaginative mind set to work again, and very soon found the answer to the problem. The answer was a simple variant of one that had already worked miraculously. The Scots had been flattered to death, very often literally, when invited to put on tartan kilts or tartan trousers and fight for the English in Europe, Asia, and America. The new variant of this old flattery was to ask them to put on bowler hats, sun topees, fur helmets, sou'-westers, or palm leaves, and fight for the English in the commercial markets of the world. And, in order to gloss over satisfactorily the essential core of the scheme, a new word had to be brought into everyday circulation. Everything in future was to be called British, and upon the extent to which the Scots could be induced to accept this new word depended the whole success of the scheme of flattery.

The Scots accepted it, hook, line, and sinker, and the scheme worked to perfection.

The industrial revolution spread all across the world and the opportunities for ambitious young Scots spread with it. They were no longer tied to the neighbourhood of Glasgow, and they followed trade wherever it ramified across the Seven Seas, and they were enormously   successful. Their ancestral toughness of spirit, and their ancestral capacity for hard work, a quality that is vitally essential for a poverty-stricken country, and their wide book-learning, made them ideal salesmen and ideal buyers. But it was these very qualities that kept them to their desk and their books. Their cautious methodical eyes were fixed on their ledgers, and while their ambitious souls were burning to reach the next rung on the ladder, the English were casually jotting down a few figures in a few ledgers and going by short cuts to the top rung of the ladder. It is characteristic of the Scot that he should be incomparably the finest bank-clerk in the world. But what are the names of the heads of the banks? Are they not apt to be names like Pease, Goodenough, Baring or Hambro, or Rothschild, Stern or Montagu Norman?

The Scots have methodically built up the great jute trade between Dundee and Calcutta, and many another trade, but it was an Englishman who saw in a moment of poetical genius the significance of Singapore, and another who had the dream of an all-red route from Capetown to the Mediterranean, and a third whose vision made the American republic and saw, even in the misery of Valley Forge, that it must be free to stretch from coast to coast. Wherever the Scot went he looked for opportunities for trade. Small profits and quick returns was his idea. The English looked for trade but for imperial expansion as well, because they took the long view that a man who could be content with no profits and no returns for a long time, might ultimately find that infinite wealth was flowing in.

It followed, however, from the natural qualities of the Lowlanders that they could not all remain bank-clerks. They were bound to rise in their professions, especially in those professions when they had to compete with the more easy-going, less short-sightedly ambitious, southerner. If two men are working side by side in a counting-house, and one of them is determined to become the managing-director of the counting-house and the other is determined to rule the world, it is probable that the former will rise to the managing-directorship sooner than the latter. But whether he will not in the end find himself under the dominion of the latter is another affair.

It has been especially in colonial and native administration that the Scots have excelled, because their geographical and financial position in the world has never given them the superiority-complex which begins by aweing and ends by alienating subject races, and thus they have been outstandingly successful in reaching and, having reached, in administering vice-royalties, governor-generalships, governorships, commissionerships, and so on. This talent for securing a number of high places out of proportion to their numbers might have infuriated a less wise race than the English. It is a talent that has been disastrous down the ages to the Jews — indeed it is the father and mother of all pogroms — and in recent times to the Armenians. But the English have been wise enough, and clever enough, to turn the position to double advantage to themselves. They have seen, of course, that it is very nice to have so much of their empire efficiently governed for them. Why should the sons of Eton and St James's Street leave the three-mile radius, and Lord's and Ascot, and — most ironical hit of all — the grouse-moors, the deer-forests, and the salmon-rivers of Scotland — to go and swelter in Madras, freeze in South Georgia, or catch some particularly nasty disease in Sierra Leone, when the sons of Aberdeen and Glasgow will go and do it for them? So the sons of Eton and St James's Street did not at first complain. They were getting a good bargain, just as they had got a good bargain with the soldiers and the traders, and they knew it. But the next development of their scheme was positively uncanny in its brilliance. It was good policy not to complain about the excess of Scots in high places. Would it not be even better policy to raise a bogus complaint? Would it not be even more paying to raise clenched fists to heaven and call down maledictions on these brilliant, talented, learned, ubiquitous Scots who "run the British Empire"?

And so it was done.

A second legend was created which was to supersede the first. The first legend had laid down the doctrine that the English Empire was British. The second laid down the doctrine that the British Empire was Scots.

It worked like a charm. The Celts, perhaps the most easily flatterable race in the world, fell into the trap and redoubled their labours as empire-builders and traders. They smirked over their success. They got together in corners and told each other stories in the vernacular about, "heids of departments," and they drank each other's healths in such toasts as, "Here's tae us, fa's like us, damn a few, and they're a' deid." They sneered loudly at the poor unsuccessful English and, when their sneers were mildly received, repeated them with an added one about spinelessness.

The three things which the Celts did not notice about the new legend were, firstly, that it made them work harder than ever for England, and especially for London; secondly, that it effectively stifled any latent discontent that might still survive from the Union of the Parliaments, and any faint desire that might have arisen for Home Rule, and any feeling of humiliation at being governed by another country; and thirdly, that it simply was not true.

Take the three points in order:

Firstly, it is only human nature to work harder for a thing if you feel that it belongs to you. It is true that there is such a thing as pride of work, but there is also such a thing as pride of possession, and the greatest results are bound to be attained when the two go together. The famous Scottish governors governed more famously than ever for the Empire which the ships of the Anglo-Saxon had taken from the armies and navies of the world, and the Scottish tradesmen heaped up more and more money on which to pay income-tax and super-tax, and on which to pay commissions as it passed backwards and forwards through the clearing-houses of London.

Secondly, the feeling of humiliation at being governed by another country, which certainly existed at the time of the Union in 1707 and for years afterwards, and which ought to have continued to exist until it was wiped out as Bruce wiped it out, had steadily declined, as we have seen, as the cash advantages of the Union increased. Now it was totally destroyed for generations by the legend. "Scotland is no longer governed by England, but England is governed by Scotland," was one of the tenets of the legend. Another was, "It is nothing that the Westminster Parliament absorbed the Edinburgh Parliament; the crux is that the Stuart's throne absorbed the Tudor." Another was, "The Stone of Destiny is once again in the possession of the Celts, its rightful owners."

The moment all these slogans were accepted by a gullible race, the thin corpse of Scottish Nationalism was burnt on a funeral pyre from which not even the tail-feather of a phoenix was visible for many a long year. The consciousness of a national pride, the longing to preserve all that is best of the past while accepting whatever may be good of the present, the passionate desire to belong to a country which thinks for itself and does not accept the thoughts which are manufactured for it elsewhere and despatched to it through the three-halfpenny post, all these begin in the hearts of a nation's poets and writers. And when the hearts of a nation's poets and writers are dead, then you may be sure that these national desires are dead too. Scotland, during the last sixty or seventy years of the nineteenth century, and in spite of the revival of the previous century, produced less literature than any other country in Western Europe. Look at the horrors which were being done to

England during that period, both in the countryside and behind the shadow of the aspidistra, and look what a cyclonic outburst of literary creation coincided with it. While Scotland was producing the footling Kailyard school — so aptly named, for no vegetable was ever duller than kail, and no piece of ground more dreary than the "yard" — and a few anglicised products like Stevenson and Lang, England was tumbling out its cataract of genius. Of scholars there were plenty in Scotland, and of doctors and surgeons and scientists, but these are men who ply an international trade. They belong to no native national school.

And so it was also with the celebrated school of painters who are known as the Glasgow school.

The plastic and pictorial arts seldom express the soul of a nation. Mestrovic may have succeeded in conveying the nasty crudeness of the Serbian character, and Gaudi, the architect of the cigar-shaped towers of the Barcelona cathedral, certainly represents the anarchy of urban Catalonia, and the bungalow is certainly typical of what might be called the spirit of British India, in its widest sense. But these are exceptions. On the whole the painters and sculptors and architects have not been national. They may have created beauty for the sake of beauty, like the men who made the temple of Segesta or the Parthenon, or for the sake of cash, like Benvenuto Cellini, or for a woman, or for religion, like the early painters of the Renaissance, or for the sake of pure mathematics, or even, in the ultimate and desperate and nineteenth-century resort, for art's sake. But they took no part in nationalism, nor did they ever.

That is why the Glasgow school of painting could flourish and become famous, where there was no native Scottish school of literature. The hand of England had fallen upon the one. It could not fall upon the other, because the other was, as painting always is, international. A picture of Christ is a picture of Christ whether it is painted by Raphael or a man called Ap Jones. But a wild poem for liberty is Italian if it is written by Mazzini, and German if by Körner, and Polish if by Mickiewicz.

So the Glasgow school went on painting, but no one wrote the wild poems for Scottish liberty.

With Scotland's absorbment into England's commercial enclosure, Scotland's national aspirations went into the shades, and Scotland's literature went with them. Rich men became more plentiful than poets.

And the third point about this legend, which the English invented, was, as I have said, that it was not true. At no time have the English oligarchy ever allowed the control of their destinies, or anything remotely approaching the control of their destinies, to pass out of their hands. On only two occasions since the days of Cromwell have they even seemed to let it pass out of their hands, and on both these occasions it was only a semblance and not a reality. The first occasion was the formation of the first Labour Government, with Liberal support, in 1924, and the second was the formation of the second, in 1929. Each time it appeared to the world that the English oligarchy had at last faltered and that its long flourishment had come to the yellow leaf at last. And each time the world did not understand that the English oligarchy does not depend simply upon a majority of votes in the House of Commons. True, it likes to have such a majority, and the bigger the better. It will pour out money in hundreds of thousands of pounds each year, even when no election is being fought, in order to buttress and increase, or, if the worst has happened, to recapture that majority. But it has other reserves behind that façade of power. Not for nothing was the Duke of Wellington the greatest of all tactical defensive fighters, also the greatest of all English oligarchs. His method of defence in the battlefield was to draw up as thin a line of men as he could risk, within view of the enemy, and to keep all the rest as much out of sight as possible, in reserve and in hidden reserve and in rearguard reserve. As with the Duke, so with the oligarchy. The votes in the House of Commons are its thin line on the crest of the ridge, in full view, equipped with skirmishers, heavy guns, light guns, and a little cannon-fodder. Behind this line are the reserves.

Let us imagine that we have the advantage over Marshal Masséna, the Prince of Essling, who had no means of knowing how Wellington had disposed his forces on the ridge of Bussaco, in Spain, in 1810, because the Marshal-Prince had no aeroplane and could not look over the top of the ridge. Let us imagine that we are attacking the universal English Wellington, the symbolical oligarch, and that we have an aeroplane with which to survey his position, and especially his reserves. In the first reserve there is only a sprinkling of men, but they are very important because they are a nucleus. They are a shadow force, a cadre, which can be filled in an emergency to a prodigious size, and which, on occasion, can turn out in a wonderful medieval uniform of fur and ribbon and crown. This is called the House of Lords. It is true that the Conservative part, which is about ninety per cent. of the House of Lords, is apt to come hobbling up to the rescue on false alarums, such as the recent revolutionary idea of stopping the torturing of rabbits in steel traps, and it is true that if it is told, with particular and unoligarchic sharpness to go away from the battlefield, as it was in 1910, it will meekly go away. But as a general rule it can be relied upon to stand in the breach if the front line is pierced. Behind the Lords we can see many other bodies of reserves, hidden away in the folds of the Chilterns and Cotswolds and Malverns and Pennines and in many other unexpected places.

Down there in a particularly unpleasant amateur-Gothic building at the end of a street that is densely populated with Scotsmen, and called, with unintentional but none the less terrible irony, by the same name as the Fleet Prison, we can see the dry forms of men in horse-hair wigs and scarlet and ermine robes. They are trying as hard as men can try to be neutral, but they are oligarchic in birth and oligarchic in idea. They have been brought up in, and have made their money in, and occupy their present position in, the defence of the Law, not of the Law as it might be in an ideal world, but of the Law as it is in England.

Behind them is a lesser and larger crowd of men in wigs, seated upon benches, all doing the same, in their own light, as the men in scarlet and ermine. And behind them again, we can see from our aeroplane a vast army of oligarchic reserves, also sitting on benches, but not wearing wigs or gowns. These are the amateur judges. Where the others, in the High Court and County Courts, are the regular soldiers, these are, literally, the territorials, and in the courts of quarter sessions and petty sessions, they form a solid bulwark of English reserves.

Then there are the diplomats, the civil servants, the officers in the navy and the army and the air force, the schoolmasters of the Public Schools. They are all concealed in the slopes of the ground. Rather less well-concealed are the major-generals and vice-admirals in the clubs. And there is the great host of rich men who command servants and votes. And behind all these are still two more lines. One is perhaps the most powerful of all, and it certainly covers the entire region of the back-areas behind the Duke of Wellington's thin red line, and the other is the most skilfully concealed and is the key-reserve upon which all the potential manoeuvring of all the rest depends.

Look down from our reconnoitring aeroplane upon the back-areas where the enemy would be likely to put the horse-lines of his cavalry, and here we see at once that the countryside is covered with horses. We can almost hear them whinnying as the cavalry charge is sounded. Or is it perhaps not a cavalry charge but a Tally-ho, or a Gone-away? We are too high above them so we shall never know. But what is that crowd of little creatures, looking like the Shape of God reduced to the size of a slug, that busies itself hither and thither among the horses of the cavalry reserve? Some are black, some red. Whenever we catch a glimpse of their upturned faces, we can vaguely see that the faces of the red-coated men are red and fat, and that the faces of the black-coated men are pale and thin. But although the details are vague, as we are flying at a great height, we can just make out that around the horses, the black and the red are working as closely together as if they had been the two essential components of a roulette board instead of, as they are, "those pillars of the English State, the Parson and the Squire."

And last of all, hidden, yet present in every mind, motionless but the mainspring, is the Court of St James's and all that those five words mean.

And all that is the Duke of Wellington's defensive army, drawn up behind its slopes, in echelon, each unit ready to support its neighbour, each unit ready to cover an exposed flank, each unit ready to retreat for a moment in good order and then, on the word, to halt, wheel about in perfect drill, and hold its place in the scheme of general defence, or to fight its way back to its original position, and all, in the ultimate crisis, but never until the ultimate crisis, ready to move forward together to the counter-attack that cannot be resisted.

And that, Scottish gentlemen, is the country you pretend to rule. That is the land of which you claim to be masters.

On what do you base this claim of yours, this claim which has arisen in the last fifty years? Upon some business men, some generals, an admiral, two archbishops, six prime ministers, an infinity of journalists, an infinity of chartered accounts, and, earlier than fifty years ago, a couple of dozen governor-generals.

The governor-generals I grant you. Dalhousie was a great man, and Minto was probably as great as the English Milner, and there were many who could at least have held a candle to the English Cromer or John Lawrence.

The business men are not only no better at business than the Londoners, but could not even exist without the Londoners. The generals were mostly failures, and none rose above mediocrity.

The Admiral was Sir Rosslyn Wemyss who signed the Armistice on behalf of the British Empire in Marshal Foch's train in the Forest of Compiègne, on November 11th, 1918. But if there had been any justice in the world Sir Rosslyn's place at the Armistice table would have been taken by the Englishman who alone of all men had made the victory possible, Admiral of the Fleet Lord Jellicoe.

As for your six Prime Ministers, Gladstone was the son of a Liverpool millionaire and he was educated at Eton and Oxford; Lord Rosebery was educated at Eton and Oxford; Sir Henry Campbell-Bannerman was a Highlander, a Campbell of Stracathro, and at least was educated at Glasgow before being sent to Cambridge, but he was a cosmopolitan to the finger-tips and preferred to speak French even in his own family circle; Lord Balfour was educated at Eton and Trinity, and was a perfect product of the culture of the world; Bonar Law was much nearer to the soil of Scotland in that he was a "son of the manse," but the manse was in Canada, and when Bonar Law did come to Scotland it was to become an ironmaster in Glasgow; only the sixth was born of the people and retains the accent of the people. But however proud you may be of Mr Ramsay Macdonald, it is a tall order that you would base your claims to intellectual dominance and political sagacity upon his achievements.

So it boils down to newspaper men and chartered accountants and a couple of archbishops.

* * *

Of course, the whole idea is balderdash from beginning to end. No one except a very vain and very gullible Scot would really believe that he ruled the destinies of the fat, sleek lands of England, that he was the master of those red-brick villages, of those grey stone towns, of those carved cathedrals, of those downs and meadows and smug antiquity. No one but a very vain and gullible Scot would stand three-quarters of the way up a dung-heap in Lombard Street and flap his wings and crow that he was King not only of the castle but of all the lands round, which he had never seen. "This noble realm of England," said the Earl of Salisbury more than five hundred years ago, "hath been a long season in triumphant flower." Yes, and the flower is not withering yet. But there are Scots people who really believe that the English have surrendered the guardianship of the flower. When the Earl of Salisbury said those words it was not so very long since England had fought its first naval battles at Sluys and Les Espagnols-sur-Mer. From the days of those battles the English have never trusted in any man or in anything for their security except in their own sailors and their own ships. Yet there are Scots who really believe that suddenly, after five centuries, the English have handed over the control of their realm to an unmaritime nation.

It would be fantastic if it were not true.

And it would be amusing if it were not dangerous.

For this legend is one of the most insidious enemies that the Scots have ever had to deal with. It has lured them into a false confidence that is based on nothing. They are like a general who is under the impression that he has captured the key-point of the enemy defences and who, if he had the sense to look for one moment over his shoulder, would see that his own communications have been cut and that the enemy is already entrenched in his capital. They are in even worse condition than that. They are like a general who has been at last persuaded to look over his shoulder and see for himself that the enemy is entrenched in his capital, and who merely remarks: "I know all about that. They are my prisoners."

Scotland today has marched out her modern flowers of the forest and sent them to the illusory capture of an inexpugnable fortress. Her soldiers of talent and courage are scattered in a thousand outposts round the world, each firmly under the impression that he is a conquering invader, If he looked over his shoulder for one instant, he would see that Edinburgh has fallen long since. Rupert's horsemen at Edgehill and Naseby galloped victoriously through the parliamentarian soldiers and came back too late, to find the battle irretrievably lost. In the American War between the States, 1861-1865, the Federal Commander, Pope, was pushing forward in great style when he saw tall, black columns of smoke rising into the hot Virginian air and heard from furiously riding despatch-carriers that Stonewall Jackson himself was astride his communications and was burning his depot at Manassas Junction. The first that General Mack, snug at Ulm in 1805, heard about the movements of Napoleon was that the French had straddled the Danube at Ingolstadt, between Ulm and Vienna, and that there was nothing left for him to do but to surrender.

But the English were more skilful than to demand a surrender. Confident in the twin forces of their own poetical skill at flattery and their victims' infinite depths of gullibility, they left the trap wide open. They did not burn the depot to make an ostentatious column of smoke in the air; they did not close the teeth of the pincers as Napoleon closed them after Bernadotte's corps of the Grande Armée had seized the Danube crossing at Ingolstadt. They simply lay back in their armchairs in White's, Brook's, Boodle's, or the Carlton, and smiled the immemorial smile of the cat, which is all the more sinister because no one has ever seen it.

And all the time Edinburgh, Edinburgh has fallen.

CHAPTER XVI

The Character of the Lowlander

Now what manner of man is it who has emerged from this brief survey of the history of the South of Scotland, and in whose hands lies the destiny and the future of the land?

What is this Lowlander?

I will begin by writing down three of the things which he is not, but which he is usually supposed to be. The Lowlander has not a universal inferiority complex. It is the custom of the English to say that he has, and it has come to be accepted as a truism. The English, of course, only say it among themselves: in public they stick to their legend that the Scot is the greatest man on earth. But it must be remembered that the English are under the impression that the whole world is wildly jealous of them and is, therefore, suffering from this complex. It is certainly true that few races would have so strong an excuse for an inferiority complex as this small, poor, lonely Lowland race, living on the borders of the rich and arrogant English. Other races have succumbed to the complex in the same circumstances. It is, for example, this neighbourhood of the rich and arrogant land of France which has made Germany the insanely jealous land which she is. But the Lowlander has not allowed the complex to master him. Indeed it would be out of keeping with his nature if he did. For any sort of complex means a surrender in some measure to unrealism; it means believing something which is slightly off the plumb; it means getting the perspective wrong.

Now if I have sketched the outline of any character at all in this historical survey, it surely must be the character of a realist. The moss-trooper, the medieval murderer, the destroyer of cathedrals, and Macandrew the engineer, had the one common quality. They were practical. The world they lived in might be a wrong one; it very often, I think, was a wrong one, but it was always a real one. Somewhere or other in the long journey from Poitou or beyond, the Celtic Picts shed their Celtic twilight, and Edward Plantagenet did the rest. The Lowlander's lack of poetry; his belief in book learning; his skill with ledgers; his refusal to retreat from lost battlefields are all part of a realist's mind. Poetry is useless; books are written to be studied; figures must be added up correctly; soldiers are made to conquer or die. It is all true to a pattern.

Of course, this intense realism is not proof against human vanity, but then nothing in the world is proof against that most amiable of weaknesses. So when you tell a Lowlander, as the English have so subtly told him for the last fifty years, that he is a greater man than he actually is, he very naturally believes you. But if you tell him that he is a smaller man than he actually is, his stern sense of realism rises at once to the surface, and he very naturally declines to believe you.

Again, people will say that the Lowlander has no sense of humour. This has been handed down from father to son in England, ever since the first original statement was made by a very silly English parson called Smith. This parson, the Reverend Sydney, was by way of being a wit. Some of his wittiest sayings have, most unfortunately for him; been handed down. They are not earth-shakers. But it was this reverend epigrammatist who started the idea about the Scots and their sense of humour, and the world has continued to believe it, It is a strange phenomenon that a race which has provided some of the subtlest and driest humour of the last half-century should have been universally labelled as humourless on the advice of the race which has produced Punch, but so it is. If you do not split your sides in a gentlemanly way over the Reverend Smith's type of witticism, then you have no sense of humour. That is the argument. The truth lies, of course, in the other platitude which has had such an uphill battle to fight against Smith's "surgical operation" line, and which is that the Lowland Scot will not bother to laugh at poor jokes. Being a realist, he has neither leisure nor inclination to pretend an amusement which he does not feel. The Highlander will laugh at anything, partly out of a natural love of laughter, and partly out of courtesy. Any excuse is good enough for him to extract a little gaiety from the mad world, and no excuse is good enough for hurting the feelings of a story-teller. But the Lowlander has no time to waste in faking gaiety or soothing susceptibilities. He is in a hurry to pass on to the next thing and forget the last.

The third of the three great fallacies about the Lowlander is that he is avaricious. Here, again, all that we have to do is to apply the yard-stick, and the fallacy becomes obvious. The realist takes a realistic view of money. That is all. Scotland has been in the past a desperately poor country. With immense exertion and sacrifice, she has acquired a certain amount of prosperity, and, because of those exertions and sacrifices she naturally values the prosperity more highly than if it had been more easily won. The corollary is a rooted antipathy to waste. The English, with their easy money flowing in from all parts of the world, are by nature wasteful. They have become careless about money, and in the passage of time they have come to regard carelessness as a synonym for generosity or lordliness. But "Easy come, easy go" is not really based upon an inherent generosity. It is based upon the subconscious conviction that "there is plenty more where that came from." In other words, "The Lord will provide," and, the Lord being an Englishman, rightly so.

But it is very different in Calvinistic Scotland. For one thing, the Lord is not a Scotsman. He is a stern old gentleman from the neighbourhood of Sinai. For another, his past record of provision for Scotland has been a very poor one, and does not for a moment justify optimism for the future if he is left to his own devices. It was not until the Scot took a hand in the business and abandoned theology somewhat for commerce that provision began to flow into the country, and the Scot does not intend to revert to the old unsatisfactory situation.

Thus he is resolute against carelessness with money, because carelessness is waste. But the English, not in the least understanding that anyone can ever have been really poor, and mixing up the two distinct qualities, only sees a lack of financial lordliness. From this germ comes the legend of avarice. The Lowlander is careful of his bawbees, not in order to hoard them in a stocking, but in order to wait until he can find something worth buying.

You have only to look at appeals for charity in Scotland, at endowments of universities, at the building of hospitals, to see the truth of this. During the war, for instance, Aberdeen, traditionally supposed to be the toughest of a tough lot of cities, raised more money per head of population for war-charities than any other city in the whole of the United Kingdom. When the cause is a good one, when there is a realistic reason for the giving of money, there is no man more lavish or more generous than the Lowlander.

* * *

We have seen how individualism, violence, and realism were forced upon the Lowlander, and these three qualities permeate his character. They make him impatient of sham, which is good, but they make him carry his impatience a logical step farther and make him impatient of uselessness, which is not so good. For uselessness includes poetry and dreams. An osprey is useful because its feathers can be sold, but the reflection of an osprey in still water is quite useless, and therefore to be ignored. The Lowlander is direct in thought and speech and deed, and this is often mistaken for bad manners. In a sense, of course, it is bad manners. But in another sense it is the perfection of manners, for it cuts out all the fripperies, and exposes at once a complete sincerity. The elegant courtesy of the Highlander may conceal anything from hatred to boredom. The one thing that probably does not underlie it is an elegant courtesy. But the shattering bluntness of the Lowlander means that you are not being deceived. Without the waste of a moment he shows you what is in his mind. You may not like his method, but you must admire his unflinching integrity of thought. He values his own sincerity more then he values your praise. His manners bring him enemies, but enemies have never been so repugnant to him as frippery. He has been more at home for centuries in a foray than in a minuet, and it is only in the last fifty years that he has begun to listen to the siren-song of the English, pouring into his ear the subtle tale of infinite greatness and imperialism.

Will the last fifty years cancel all the centuries? That is really the point. Are the Lowland Scots so changed that they will meekly allow to be destroyed all that their ancestors saved?

I do not believe that they have changed an iota. But I do believe that the Lowland character may, with perfect consistency to itself, take either of two diametrically different courses in this modern era. It would be in complete harmony with the story of the past, if the Lowlander decided to recapture Edinburgh and make Scotland a nation once again. Nationalism has been in the ascendant ever since the end of the World War, and the Scots may suddenly feel the deep urge for a free Scotland which kept them alive from 1292 until the Union of the Parliaments.

But there is another course, and it is just as logical. The Lowlander may turn his back completely and for ever on the past, and restlessly face the future, seeking some new thing. And for Scotland that new thing can only be the ultimate absorption in the mighty England. The Lowlander may decide that this is best, and that what has once gone should never be resuscitated.

It is for those who believe in Scottish Nationalism to convince the Lowlander, who is and has been for five hundred years the strength of the country, that the first course is the best, and that Edinburgh ought to be recaptured.

CHAPTER XVII

Three Questions

Three questions more, and I have finished.

One: Is Edinburgh worth recapturing?

Two: Are we likely to try to recapture it?

Three: Can it be recaptured?

The first question: Is Edinburgh worth recapturing?

Is the freedom of Scotland worth having? By the word freedom I do not mean that Scotland should insist, as De Valera is tenaciously insisting for Ireland, upon a complete severance. The Irish Gael is, politically, far in advance of the Scottish Gael, and what he has fought for, we have not fought for; what he has already won, we have not even begun to beg; and his aims, so nearly consummated, are far beyond us at the moment.

By the word freedom, in this context, I mean an intellectual freedom through political self-government. Economic self-government is no longer possible for anyone within range of London. That must be excluded at once from any consideration of Scotland's future. All financial and economic roads lead to London. We are all a Hudson's Bay Company.

But political self-government is another matter. Egypt has just received it. So have the Philippines, and Iraq; the French Syrian mandate is about to get it; I rather fancy the Hedjaz has it; Haiti and San Domingo certainly have it.

But is it worth while, this political independence? That is the point.

I think the answer lies in a queer kink of human nature. History has shown over and over again that almost every nation would sooner govern themselves badly, corruptly, incompetently, than be efficiently governed by an alien. A nation may be suppressed by alien dominance for four hundred years, as Bulgaria was by Turkey, for example, and still retain the spirit and the determination, and enough poets, to get free at last. From the point of view of worldliness, it would often be in the interest of the subject race to go on being subjects. Good government is a jewel. But there is something in Western human nature — for it does not apply to the East with anything like the same force — which makes it regard self-government as a jewel, and alien-government as a devil. There is no rational explanation of this. It would be more reasonable to suppose that the small man, the little tradesman, the clerk, the garage-hand, the shorthand typist, the street-walker, would not care two straws who worked the governmental machine, provided that it was worked in such a way that they did not suffer undue inconvenience — in other words, provided that it was worked efficiently.

But human nature is far otherwise.

Human nature, as it is now, is tending more and more towards national political independence. The very word "political" is derived from the Greek word which means a city, and if ever there were units which fought to the death for self-government they were the Greek city-states.

To be a free man is to be able to hold up your head among free men.

That is a very desirable thing to be able to do. But the argument goes further.

To be the citizen of a nation which might be free, but is not free owing to external compulsion, means that you cannot hold up your head among free men quite so high as they hold theirs. But to be the citizen of a nation which might be free, but does not want to be free, means that you cannot properly associate with free men at all in places where the old idea of the city-state, which we now call political freedom, is held in esteem. A slave, as a slave, is to be pitied. A slave who does not want to escape, is to be despised. All free men will despise him.

In a book published some years ago, Major A. J. Evans, the England cricketer, described his experiences in trying to escape from German prison camps during the war. The book was called *The Escaping Club*, and a very exciting book it was. In it Major Evans said that there was a distinct line to be drawn between those prisoners of war who acquiesced in their captivity, and those restless spirits who never ceased for a moment in the planning, and, when possible, in the execution of schemes of escape. Those who acquiesced sank into a mental lethargy which sooner or later began to affect their minds. Those who ceaselessly plotted and planned kept their balance. They had something to live for, and they lived for it.

It might, of course, be argued the other way round; that the sort of man whose whole soul is not set upon liberty does not sink into a mental lethargy, because he is there already; and that the sort of man who must be free and will endure anything to obtain freedom can never lose his balance because his mind is too fine and too high for silly stupidities. But whichever way round you look at it, the conclusion is the same. He who wants to be free, is alive. He who does not, is dead.

* * *

In a moment or two I am going to quote Mr George Malcolm Thompson that the Union of the Parliaments no longer pays us a dividend. It used to bring us money. It does so no longer.

But that is only a lever to move inertia. It is, like Jaques' Ducdame in *As You Like It*, simply "an invocation to call fools into a circle." I am not advocating Home Rule for Scotland simply on the ground that it will pay us better in cash, although I am quite certain that it will.

I am advocating it because I believe that Scotland today has a unique chance of creating an enclave of sanity and culture in a world gone mad. I am advocating it because I believe that no other part of the world has the same opportunity, or anything like the same opportunity, of making a constructive stand against the rising tide of barbarism. And it is rising as fast as the tide ever rose on Solway.

Wherein lies the uniqueness of the opportunity?

There are several factors, each of which would encourage any race less complacent than the Lowlander or less defeatist than the Highlander to work for political independence, which make Scotland's position today so extraordinary. Let us briefly see what advantages Scotland has for the creation of something in an era when all else seems bent on destruction.

She is small. The modern state is becoming more and more top-heavy. It is too big. The grandiosity — *folie des grandeurs* of Napoleon — is gaining ground every day. The talk is all of federations, and amalgamations, and alliances, in industry, finance, and politics. And the only result is unwieldiness. But Scotland is small. She is not unwieldy, but a compact country in which most of the population live within a few hours' railway journey of each other. This smallness is an advantage which she shares with Estonia, San Marino, Andorra, and England.

But England has the disadvantage of an enormous population for her size, so, although small geographically, she is, politically and socially, monstrous.

Scotland is very well educated. I detest the division of people into "classes," but it is very difficult to find a set of words which will so adequately and so compactly convey the meaning which I am trying to convey, as those dreadful phrases, "working-classes," "lower middle-classes," etc. etc. They are dreadful, but they do simplify explanations. So I must continue that Scotland's working-classes are as well-educated as England's. Certainly not better, but certainly not worse. The middle-classes and upper-classes, that is to say the well-to-do bourgeois and the gentry, are probably not so well-educated as the

English. In particular the gentry is apt to be provincial. But where Scotland has an enormous, incalculable pull over every country in the world, is in her "lower middle-classes" and in her professional standards.

The factory worker, the farm-labourer, the policeman, the shop-assistant, the newspaper-seller, may be of little education. But their sons may become anything.

That section of the Scottish people which has just emerged from slumdom — and has emerged entirely by its own efforts and ambitions — but has not yet attained to the solidity of the bourgeoisie, is a fascinating study. It is there that the indomitable — I make no apology for using that word so often about the Lowlander: after all, it only means untameable — passion for education lies. It is in that "lower middle-class" that you get the burning of the midnight candles. Thence came many of the great scholars, and almost all the mechanics, and very many of the ministers whose sons in their turn left the manse and helped to make the English Empire.

The gentry, as we know them now, have been anglicised a long time. The middle-classes were made by the nineteenth century. But this passionate desire for knowledge, which distinguishes Scotland from the rest, is part of the passionate heritage of Scotland's poor.

Consider one example.

David Kirkwood was a working engineer on the Clyde. He was one of thousands who drove rivets or welded plates, or whatever it is that working engineers do. You will find them at Woolwich, at Devonport, Chatham, on the Tees, Wear, Tyne, and in Belfast, and in many other places. They are all small men, of humble origin, and very small education.

Kirkwood educated himself. He has been for years one of the best parliamentarians in the House of Commons. God gave him ability. He has given himself knowledge. He is the type of what I mean, the type of Scotsman who is resolute to extract himself from the misery into which the industrial revolution forced his grandparents. I know nothing like it, on such a scale, elsewhere.

Then there is Scotland's second asset — her professional standard.

In engineering, accountancy, banking, the law, and above all in medicine, the Scottish standard is high. There is a tradition of integrity now which has long since outmoded the old tradition of treachery and savagery. And, according to the usual practice of the Lowlander, he is as vehement now in his integrity as he used to be in his earlier customs.

Thus, in the matter of education, Scotland possesses one class far ahead of any other corresponding class in the world; the rest not particularly inferior to any others; and in proportion to population an unparalleled body of professional skill. Those qualities rule out comparison with Estonia, San Marino, and Andorra.

Another of Scotland's assets is England's comparative good will. I say, comparative, because England's economic and financial policy towards Scotland during the last decade and a half has shown very little good will at all. On the other hand, for the last hundred years or so England's general tolerance has been a good deal more marked towards Scotland than towards, say, Ireland or the Boer Republics. Not since 1746 has black-and-tannery been let loose in the glens.

Scottish Home Rule, therefore, would have the immense advantage of being born into an atmosphere that is entirely free from the bitterness of political murder, terrorism, ambush, concentration-camp, informer, and execution, and reprisal. In this Scotland would have the advantage over Poland, as well as over Ireland and the Union of South Africa.

There would be no humiliation in the acceptance of the English fleet to defend the shores of Scotland, for it would be the fleet of a friend. Rosyth, Invergordon, and Scapa would be lent with the utmost cordiality as naval bases without any of that bargaining and haggling which is so destructive of mutual good will.

But the greatest asset which Scotland has, an asset the like of which exists nowhere else in the world, is the potential value of Edinburgh as a capital city.

It has all the beauty of half a dozen different sorts of beautiful city. The old town has the picturesque-ness of Cracow in grey instead of in red. The squares and crescents of the new town are eighteenth century at its most elegantly dignified. Princes Street and the Calton Hill are sheer magnificence. The view from George Street over the Forth and the hills of the kingdom of Fife is pure San Francisco. And, as if that was not enough beauty and strangeness for one city, in the middle of it all is that incredible castle. To Edinburgh's beauty add Edinburgh's history. To both add her men of genius. Add her arts, her medicine, her schools; her law; her legends; her traditions. What other capital city in the world outside Rome and Athens can equal the result of all that heaping of treasure upon treasure?

But that is not yet all. Edinburgh has one other treasure left, shared still with many cities, happily, but not now with Rome and Athens, and that is freedom of thought. You may think and talk and laugh there. No secret police will stop you. There are no Lipari Islands near the Bass Rock. There is no Gestapo in Leith Walk. So of all the qualities which might go to the making of a great capital city, some have these and some have those and some have few, but only Edinburgh has them all.

Edinburgh has often been called the New Athens. It cannot be allowed to be a very happy description. Those who coined the description, and those who pass it now in currency, mean that just as Athens was supreme in the arts and in the thoughts of her day, so is Edinburgh in hers.

They are completely wrong. They ignore the deep difference. They compare two surfaces without wondering how those surfaces were created.

Athens was of all things a free city. The speeches which Thucydides put into the mouth of Pericles are like aquamarine in their clarity: political freedom is the beginning and end of all proper human life. All things are possible for a free people, even moderation and generosity. And it was on that foundation of the city-state, the *Polis*, the free political mind, that Athens built her Acropolis of creative genius.

How can Edinburgh be compared with that and called the New Athens? The framework is there, the city, the education, the history, all is there except the divine spark. Edinburgh is the greatest dead thing in the world. Athens was the greatest alive thing in the world. And if Edinburgh is to be called the New Athens, then I say we must obliterate that dull travesty and make a Newer Athens still.

Imagine this:

Suppose Scotland became once again a self-governing country, and we went back to the days before 1707. A Scottish Parliament would sit in Edinburgh. A Civil Service would be created. The city would be filled with politicians and officials. The air would be filled with political controversy. The drawing-rooms would become *salons* with metropolitan excitement where now provincial languor droops. From all parts of the country folk would flock, some to lay a grievance before their member, some to try to arrange a bit of corruption, some to see the sights. But whatever they came for, it would not matter. They would come, and they would bring excitement. A delegation to Westminster from, say, Glossop or Merthyr Tydfil does not make a big impression upon the life of London. But a delegation from Aberdeen would soon make itself felt in Princes Street. That is one of the advantages, as I have said, of a small population. A Parliament in Edinburgh would keep the city in an incessant state of excitement.

The result of that would be like a geometrical proposition in its inevitability. Where there is excitement, there you will find the poets gathering. For poets cannot live without it. And by poets I mean all who practise any of the arts.

The new Renaissance of Scotland would flow irresistibly into Edinburgh. Much of it is there already. But not nearly all of it. For at present it has no focus, and is dissipated. It has the impulse and the fire, but it lacks the Athens. There is no Agora, no central-meeting-place, to which it is worthwhile for a nation's youth and talent to repair for the exchange of ideas and the advancement of national aspirations.

Some of Scotland's Athenians live in Edinburgh, but some live in Glasgow, and some in Inverness, or Barra, or London. And until a Parliament sits again in Edinburgh, the talent will always be scattered. Until then, there will never be a reunion of Scotland's poets.

There is at this moment a great enthusiasm for the theatre in Scotland. It cannot be called a Renaissance, because that would imply that a dramatic movement had existed before. It never has. John Calvin has been far too strong for the theatre in the Lowlands, and, as I have shown, the Highlander's natural passion for play-acting has prevented him from play-writing. But now at last the theatre has seized the Scottish imagination, and amateur societies and professional companies are springing up on all sides. But there is no focus. There is not a live, exciting Edinburgh in which this national feeling could be concentrated.

It is the same with the writers. It is the same with the renegades.

There is nothing to return to. There is no central rallying-point. Never was there such an opportunity to create an intellectual oasis amid a world of mass-barbarism. But the opportunity will be missed, unless the Parliament returns. For how can you ask writers, and painters, and sculptors, to bury themselves in a provincial town? For that is what Edinburgh is. A provincial town, just as Dunfermline, and Bristol, and Tewkesbury are provincial towns. And where there is provincialism, there also will you find complete absence of intellectual excitement, and there also you will find almost complete absence of youth and talent and ambition.

The renegades who live in London, live there for the excitement. The living is more expensive, the city is not so beautiful, and the golf is deplorable. The country round is dotted with bungalows, and there are no mountains anywhere near, and the nearest sea is hidden by Southend and Margate. But something is happening all the time. Like the Athens of St Paul, London is always seeking something new, or at any rate is always having something new thrust upon it. "For all the Athenians and strangers which were there spent their time in nothing else, but either to tell, or to hear some new thing."

So why should we leave this London for a dead city? There is no reason.

But if we were given a reason to return to Scotland, then the renegades would come home, and when the renegades came home and Scotland's youth and genius came from all parts of Scotland to the Capital of Scotland, then Edinburgh would see such a time of excitement as only Paris has seen in the last two hundred years, and a Newer Athens would be built in a year. Then a latter-day Voltaire would be able to repeat that "in all matters of taste from the epic poem to gardening, we look to Scotland."

The world is going mad in a crazy mixture of standardised thinking and totalitarian politics. Individualism is being steadily driven into a corner by mass-production, mergers, and dictators. And what sort of world will the Lowlander find it, if individualism is crushed altogether? He will have lost the outlet for his one great quality, that great quality which preserved the independence of South Scotland between the years 1292 and 1707. And then where will he be? He will have ceased to exist as a separate race. Even the Highlander will have outlived him, in the mists and in the memories, for nothing will kill the pipe-music, or the legends, or the rebirth in Canada. But once the Lowlander allows his individualism to be taken from him, then Europe will see a thing happen which has not happened at any rate since the days of Charlemagne and the end of the Dark Ages, the extinction of a once independent and separate race.

Is it not worthwhile trying to save it, simply as a race which has done good things in the past? Is it not fifty times worthwhile trying to save it for what it might do in the future, when the saving of it could so easily be made the occasion of a renaissance of a national culture and an example of political and intellectual sanity in a world of jackboots and bombing aeroplanes, and tyranny and mass-insanity?

The second question is: "Are we likely to try to recapture Edinburgh?" Is there, in fact, a sufficient number of Scotsmen who want to see a self-governing Scotland? Is the pride in Bannockburn a real pride, or is it a music-hall joke?

The answer is that at this moment, in 1937, there is certainly not a sufficient number, and no real pride. The great mass of the middle-classes, commercial folk, solid gentry, and, in general, the agriculturist and worker, does not feel very strongly about the rebirth of the nation. The figures of the Nationalist vote at elections show that clearly. The choice now is between a silly, easy provincialism and the difficult but fascinating task of re-making a metropolitan atmosphere, and massed inertia will always cling fast to the silly and the easy.

Whether or not this mass can be swung back from the music-hall to a proud place among free nations, is the issue.

Now it cannot be expected that this central block of inertia should arouse itself quickly. The influence of England is strong, and the flattering legends about Scottish superiority have sunk deep. Besides, history shows that it is usually the uneducated and the overeducated who are the last to move in a national uprising. Those who have not been taught how to think, and those who have been carefully taught how to think only in a narrow groove, are the most difficult to convert.

The essential beginning of all national uprisings is that the poets should believe. The young men and women, the writers, painters, dramatists, actors, sculptors, architects, they are the key to freedom. If they do not believe, then nothing can be done. And if they do not believe, then they are engaged in wrong professions. For they will never be poets in any art, and would fare better in the national trade of adding up figures.

The Scottish Nationalist Movement has begun at the right end. It has not begun as a political dodge or a commercial ramp, but as the spontaneous outburst of the young creators of art and beauty, whom we may call generally "poets" from the Greek word which means simply "makers."

A handful of Scottish poets declared for Scottish independence a good many years ago, and it has grown steadily in size and intellectual vigour until it includes practically every single man and woman who is contributing to the literary and artistic revival of the land.

No one expected that the rest would follow at once. History shows that public opinion is seldom less than a whole generation behind the poets; often it is much more. The man in the street cannot see as clearly, or think as far ahead, as the poet. If he could, he would be a poet too.

But history shows also that the man in the street will inevitably follow the poet in the long run unless the poet has been murdered in the meanwhile.

The politician who wants to remain perched upon his precarious throne must do one of two things to the arts. He must either woo them or kill them. Some have tried one plan, and some the other.

Monarchical France always wooed the arts and so, oddly enough, did Frederick the Great, and so did Lorenzo the Magnificent, and Charles the Second, and Haroun-Al-Raschid, and Pericles.

On the other hand, Napoleon, Mussolini, and Hitler killed them in their respective countries.

But if you do not kill your poets they will, in the end, kill you. Because the human soul is always swayed in the end by music, whether it is made out of the gut of a cat by a man called Kreisler, or whether it is jotted down on a piece of paper by a man called Shakespeare, or whether it is pumped out of an accordion in a slum by a man called Smith. For some obscure reason, or it might be called some divine reason — there is, perhaps, small difference between obscurity and divinity — the common people, and especially the men, are profoundly moved by music.

And so the politician must either shoot the poet or be defeated in the end by the mass of the common people who have listened to the poet. The moment that politics are arrayed against poetry, the decision lies between the bullet and the sonnet. And the moment that the bullet misses, the sonnet must win. There have been occasions in history when the most despicable of politicians have defeated the loveliest of poets. Cleon's foul-mouthed demagoguery was too strong for Aristophanes. On the other side of the balance-sheet, Byron was too strong for Turkey, and Gladstone, a poet at heart, defeated Neapolitan tyranny with a small series of letters.

My point is this. If you are sufficiently ruthless, you can destroy poetry by putting it up against a wall. But if you have not the nerve, or the gunmen, or the passionate desire to destroy something beautiful, to put poetry against a wall, then poetry is bound to continue, immortally.

And the people will sooner or later follow. The children of Hamelin who followed the Pied Piper are symbolic of the common people. So long as they are free to follow their choice and are not bullied by tyrants, they will follow the piper.

So the mass inertia of Scotland will swing round, slowly, perhaps very slowly, to the idea of Scottish Nationalism, because it will be forced to swing round by the young poets. They are resolute and, so long as England forgets to shoot them, their resolution must triumph in the end.

* * *

The third question: Can Edinburgh be recaptured? The answer is that it can. But the chance of a successful siege has only become possible owing to the negligence of the garrison and not at all owing to the pertinacity or opportunism of the besiegers. In the historic days when Douglas and Randolph were lying in ambush round the Scottish castles, waiting to pounce upon a single small slip of the garrison, their successes were due as much to their own vigilance as to the garrison's carelessness. But in this modern siege of Edinburgh, and of all that Edinburgh stands for symbolically, which is a free Scotland, there would have been no besiegers at all if the garrison had not made a fatal blunder.

* * *

This is what happened.

Up to the end of the fictitious trade boom of 1920, or thereabouts, the position between the English and the Scots was the same, generally speaking, as it had been for the eighty or ninety years before. That is to say, the Scots ignored every other consideration except their material prosperity, while the English went on with their normal business of collecting other people's money with one hand and with the other hand writing their own poetry. The lovely spring-flowering of poetry in the early years of the World War was pure English. Brooke, Lister, Grenfell, were English in birth and name;

Tennant, Shaw-Stewart, Sorley, Crombie, were Scottish in birth and name, but English in everything else, and Thomas and Owen were Welsh. But all were of the new Elizabethans. And of the survivors, Squire and Shanks and Turner, Graves the Welshman, Sassoon the Jew, and de la Mare the Huguenot, all are in the Elizabethan tradition. They are essentially English. But the World War produced no revival of Scottish literature. The fighting in France, Flanders, Mesopotamia, the sands of Egypt, the Holy Land, and all the corners of Armageddon, brought death and mutilation and self-sacrifice and nobility to the Scottish race, but it did not bring poetry. The new Elizabethanism brought a renaissance of gaiety to the country of Elizabeth. But it brought none to the country of James Stuart who succeeded Elizabeth. The English, supposed traditionally to be a phlegmatic, dull, stolid race, went into battle singing, as they have always done when their country was in danger, and they only stopped singing, reluctantly, when the poets had been either killed or promoted to the command of machine-gun battalions or tanks, and were so busy showing professional soldiers how to conduct their profession that they had no time to conduct their own. But the native Scots did not sing as they went into battle. There was no faint murmur of a paean such as that which the Athenian soldiers shouted when they went down towards the beach at Marathon.

But why should there have been a Scottish song? There was no land to sing for. In 1914 Scotland was financially alive, and poetically dead.

But England changed after the war. A new scion of the governing-classes had sprouted, born of dubious financial antecedents, foster-mothered by war-profits and brought up by post-war "reconstructions." Mergers and manipulations were its god-parents, and if it was christened at all, which seems, verbally at least, unlikely, it was in watered stock.

This new aristocracy was the same in outlook as Thomas Cromwell's friends who burgled the Catholic monasteries and thereby became, by the strange custom of England, aristocrats. Both the one and the other thought nothing of small profits and quick returns. What they wanted was large profits and quick returns. Then came the great trade slump in 1922.

The English merchants hastily began to draw in their horns and cut their losses. There has never yet been a man so expert in creeping under the umbrella when the blizzard is raging as your English merchant, and he has built his umbrella of the stoutest materials.

He too, like Wellington and the Oligarchy, has his reserves.

When the great slump came, the English dashed under the umbrella and waited. And then, when the worst was over, they decided to remain under the umbrella a little longer, but to call it now by a different and more dignified name. It was no longer to be a sort of funk-hole, but a Policy, and it was to be called Rationalisation.

It is a dreadful word but, as applied to Scotland by London, it has an easy, everyday, simple meaning that we can all understand. It means "dropping poor relations."

It may be described in such genteel phrases as "cutting overhead charges" or "scrapping redundant plant," or "amalgamating overlapping interests," but the result is the same. The weaker goes to the wall; goes to the poorhouse; and the naturally proud that he was fit enough the poor relation richer survivor is to survive.

Rationalisation hit Scotland a devastating economic blow.

For England, in the stress of the economic crisis, threw aside her tactful, soothing, blandishing legend, and became once again the England of Edward the Hammer. An economic blizzard, to use a picturesque and hackneyed phrase, was sweeping icily over Britain, and England was prepared, for her own safety, to sacrifice Scotland. The mask was off and little Red Riding Hood was alone in the forest with the wolf. Within a few years Scotland was shorn of her railways, and her banks, and most of her shipping. The wolf had taken them, and he went on to take a good deal more.

In the decade ending in 1931, Scotland's population fell; England's rose. Yet Scotland's birth-rate was higher. The fall was due to emigration, mostly to England, and do not let us forget that emigrants are almost always the young and the enterprising of a nation, and are usually skilful workers. And, in these modern days of drastic immigration laws in new worlds, those emigrants who go overseas are certainly not the least respectable or poorest of the citizenry. It is, in fact, the flowers of the forest that are being lost once again.

This is not a matter for controversy. The facts are known, and can be found by anyone who will take the trouble to read Mr George Malcolm Thomson's *Scotland, That Distressed Area*. Scotland's wealth is diminishing; her unemployment is high; her industries are going slowly downhill in output; in the main trades Scotland's employment is either stationary or declining; whereas, England's is sometimes stationary, but usually increasing; in all the money-making departments of the modern world, London is taking more than ever before and giving less. There is no argument possible about this. It is simply a question of looking at the facts as they are published in official documents. The money is not returning, nor are the men. What the south gets the south is apt to hold. During the worst days of the post-war slump many thousands of skilled Scottish artisans took the road to England. Now that the depression is passing away it might have been expected that Scotland would be able to reabsorb some of these men. Mr Thomson has the answer:

"We have the official Board of Trade statistics to help us here. They show that in England and Wales in 1932 there were started 626 new factories, while 130 existing factories were closed — net gain 496. In Scotland 20 new factories were opened, 36 were closed — net loss 16.

In 1933 there were 499 new factories opened in England, 380 closed — net gain 69. In Scotland 14 new factories were opened and 29 were closed — net loss 15.

At the end of these two short years, then, England had 565 more factories than at the beginning, while Scotland had 31 fewer."

So that is the ultimate result of the partnership with England. The trend of industry today is towards the south, and as the predominant partner in the union becomes relatively stronger and stronger the secondary partner becomes weaker and weaker. In 1707 Edinburgh was, in effect, sold for a steady and rising income. Now that the money is no longer being paid, surely the bargain ought to be cancelled?

* * *

The whole story of this economic policy of England during the post-war depression will have to be written some day from the point of view of the English character. Historians will have to explain why England, in a few years, suddenly began to behave in a way so completely foreign to her traditional mode. She, calmest of races, panicked; most long-sighted, she took the shortest of views; cleverest, she became silly; craftiest, she became transparently blockheaded; imperialist, parochial. But to analyse the causes for this change — not of heart, but of brain — does not come within the scope of this book. All we are concerned with is the effect of this change upon Scotland.

The effect was that England, by her unexpected and unbelievable stupidity, cut away the dyke which she had herself laboriously constructed against the possibility of a rising tide of Scottish Nationalism. She had built up the dyke of financial prosperity to keep out a flood, or anything approaching a flood, of spiritual longings. She had cleverly turned herself into a Scottish Catchment Area into which all the stray Caledonian waters should drain and be quietly eased off into the sea through locks and dams.

And then she herself cut the dyke. No one else could have done it. When England builds anything, whether it is a dyke, a pin, or an empire, it takes more than an ordinarily strong man to break it.

The only possible plea in favour of the Union of 1707 was that it would bring money to Scotland. For about two hundred years it did bring money into

Scotland. It took away government, the capital, the national status, and the spiritual pride in independence which had saved the land through centuries of adversity. It converted a country into a province. But it gave cash in return. That was the stock answer twenty years ago to any tentative suggestion of Home Rule. "Look at the money we've made." Your hard-headed realist had no desire to see Edinburgh once again a seat of government, so long as his dividends were all right. He did not care two straws for spiritual pride in independence if his companies were prospering. That was England's trump card.

The result has been inevitable. Your hard-headed realist, who goes on asking himself the same question eternally, no matter what problem he is faced with, "What do I get out of it?" has suddenly begun to find that the answer is, "Precious little." That touches him. Nothing else will. But that will. The greatest poet in the world can sing to him for hours about the splendours of freedom, and your realist will stand four-square to the winds and rattle his coins and rustle his dividend warrants, until his patience deserts him and he rings the bell for a couple of footmen to throw the poet into the street. But the story is very different when the coins dwindle and the dividends begin to pass.

That is what is happening in the Lowlands today. The poets and the writers have been alive to the situation for twenty years. They have seen that at last England, the mighty England, has bungled and has cut the dyke, and that after two hundred years the chance has come to restore Edinburgh to the same status in the world as Kovno, or Reval, or the capitals of Salvador or Nicaragua. The lever has been put in their hands at last with which to hoist laboriously, slowly, but nevertheless perceptibly, the heads of Scotland's smug industrial ostriches out of their heaps of sand. "The Union is wrong. It doesn't pay," is the chanty of the new Douglases, the latter-day Randolphs, as they heave on the capstan-bars to lift the anchor that once was made of gold, but is now being discovered to be a leaden substitute, the golden anchor having been surreptitiously carried off and deposited in the English strong box in London, beside the Stone of Destiny.

It may seem to be a sordid argument. Idealists, it may be said, like the younger generation of Scottish poets and writers, ought to use idealistic arguments and not descend into the arena. Those who wrestle with chimney-sweeps get sooty. But the days of Byron and Körner and Mickiewicz are past. The Irish poets moved the Irish nation with their songs, but they had to use murder and ambush when they met the Black-and-Tans. Sweeps must be fought with their own weapons. Lyrics will not move board meetings. Besides, soot can easily be washed off, in these days of universal plumbing.

So the young men who can write the lyrics and the prose, who are recreating a native Scottish Literature, are also digging statistics out of blue-books and compiling charts of trade-returns.

It may take years yet before their statistics and their charts begin to percolate through into the brains of commercial, and still longer into the brains of genteel, Scotland, because these people are not swift at welcoming what they themselves call "new ideas." But the new idea, that Scotland should in the twentieth century A.D. enjoy what Athens fought for at Marathon in 490 B.C., may win through yet.

Once the commercial classes and working classes can be inspired to join the cause of a free Scotland, even if the inspiration is only the rather sordid one of self-interest, then the battle is won and Edinburgh can be recaptured. England has provided the weapon. The poets are in line. All that is wanted now is to range the rest in line also.

* * *

Fundamentally, there is no half-way house between freedom and slavery. In the end there is no such thing as a free and enlightened provincialism. There can never be a partnership on equal terms between a small partner and an overwhelmingly strong one. The former must inevitably be absorbed in the end.

That is what is happening to Scotland today, and the process must either be accelerated or reversed. There is not the slightest use pretending that Scotland can survive in its present position. It is all very well for the ostrich to hide its head in the sand, but we Scots ought to remember what happens to the ostrich. He ends up in a farm where his owner plucks out his feathers and makes money by selling them.

The future lies in the hands of the Lowland Scot. It is for him to make the decision. The Highlander, as usual, has abandoned the fight and gone away. But the Lowlander still possesses his ancient violence, his individualism, and his tenacity, and somewhere deep down in his soul I believe he still possesses his patriotism. If he does, then he still has the power to recapture Edinburgh and make Scotland a nation again. But first he will have to be convinced that Edinburgh is worth recapturing.

THE END